This Song Is For You

D. MICHELLE

Copyright © 2026 by D. Michelle

All rights reserved.

No part of this book may be reproduced in any form or by any electronic or mechanical means, including information storage and retrieval systems, without written permission from the author, except for the use of brief quotations in a book review.

This is a work of fiction. Names, characters, businesses, places, events, locales, and incidents are either the products of the author's imagination or used in a fictitious manner. Any resemblance to actual persons, living or dead, or actual events is purely coincidental.

Editor: Ena Coleman

Cover Artist: Mae Rose

❀ Formatted with Vellum

Author's Note

Before you dive in...

While *This Song Is For You* is a story rooted in friendship, love, and emotional vulnerability, it does contain reflections on past and present hardships. These include: loss of loved ones, grief, alcohol abuse, mental health, and strained familial relationships.

It also includes explicit language and sexually explicit content.

If you are sensitive to any of these topics, please proceed with caution.

Playlist

To be listened to in order. Trust me, it'll make sense later!

Zhané - This Song Is For You
Michael Jackson - Butterflies
Teedra Moses - Caught Up
Tony! Toni! Toné! - (Lay Your Head On My) Pillow
Total - Kissin' You/Oh Honey
Rufus & Chaka Khan - Everlasting Love
Rahsaan Patterson - Spend the Night
Jill Scott feat. Paul Wall - So Gone (What My Mind Says)
Eric Benet - Femininity
Maxwell-Sumthin' Sumthin' (Mellosmoothe)
Trina Broussard- Inside My Love
Janet Jackson - Twenty Foreplay
Ari Lennox - Tatted
Tank - I Don't Think You're Ready
Lalah Hathaway - Angel (Live)
Mint Condition - If You Love Me
Joe - All Or Nothing
Keyshia Cole & Monica - Trust
Deborah Cox - Sentimental

Chanté Moore - It's Alright
Frankie Beverly & Maze - Can't Get Over You
D'Angelo - Really Love
Beyoncé - Plastic Off The Sofa
Tony! Toni! Toné! - Anniversary
Stevie Wonder - Ribbon In The Sky

To the yearners,

May the love that finds you feel exactly like your favorite love song.

Prologue

Melody - 2011
Sophomore Year

"Mel! You need to hurry up so we can get to this party," Tisha calls from across our dorm room. Tisha and I were assigned to each other as roommates freshman year, and luckily, we instantly clicked. Now, we're not just roommates—we're best friends.

It's our sophomore year at the University of Southern California, and tonight we're headed to a party at Cale Hall—one of the dorms on campus—being thrown by one of the seniors who runs the Black Student Assembly.

"Are you *sure* this is a costume party?" I ask as I squeeze into a tight black bodysuit. "I didn't hear anyone talking about dressing up."

I decided to be a cat because it was the easiest thing I could come up with. That, and the fact that I gained the infamous freshman fifteen pounds from all of the late-night binge eating and drinking last year. All of the weight went straight to my lower body. I'm not complaining, though. After being notoriously thin most of my life, the curves are a welcome change.

"That's what Bernard told me," Tisha confirms, interrupting my ritual over-analysis of my body. "He said there'll be a prize for the best costume."

"Bernard could tell you the sky is green and you'd believe him," I tease.

Tisha has a huge crush on Bernard. Last year, when the Black Student Assembly had a table set up in the quad trying to recruit members, he was there handing out flyers. Tisha signed *both* of us up for an upcoming event they were having, then stayed talking to him for the next fifteen minutes. They've spent the last year flirting with each other—going to lunches, meeting at the library and dining hall some evenings—neither one ever making a real move. They seem to be content hovering in that almost-something space.

"Shut up!" she laughs. "He said he really wanted me to come to the party, but told me not to say too much about it because only certain people were invited."

She adjusts her pleated skirt in the mirror and tugs her unbuttoned white collared shirt lower, exposing more of her breasts, which are already huge. Her naughty school teacher look was well executed—especially with the red lace bra peeking out from under her top.

"Let's see if you two finally do something other than debate the state of Black America and the diaspora," I say, rolling my eyes at her. When they weren't flirting, Tisha and Bernard did nothing but debate politics and history.

"I love history the way you love singing and music," she shrugs. "It's nice to have somebody who's interested in that too. And Bernard is fine as hell," she giggles.

"He is really cute, I can't lie," I agree. "I just wish you two would at least go on a proper date."

I pin my cat tail on the back of my bodysuit and put my cat ears on.

"We're building a friendship, Mel. These things take time."

"A *whole year*?!" I raise a brow. "You two are the best of friends at this point."

"Hush," she says, playfully hitting me on my shoulder.

"Everybody can't be in a committed relationship from the day they step foot onto a college campus," she adds, clearly making fun of me and Mike—my boyfriend, who I met during freshman orientation. We locked eyes during a pep rally we were supposed to be paying attention to, and we've been hooked on each other ever since.

"I'm mad Mike isn't coming tonight," I pout. "He said he has studying to do and told me just to come over after."

"Girl, I don't know why you even paid for a dorm room when you're never here," Tisha laughs. "They need to just let you and Mike split room and board."

We both crack up, putting the finishing touches on our makeup.

"I'm ready," I say, grabbing my purse.

"Let's go," she says, looping her arm through mine. "Don't worry about Mike, we're gonna have fun tonight."

Together, we make our way to the party, ready for whatever the night may bring.

When Tisha and I step off the elevator onto the 3rd floor, we immediately hear Wiz Khalifa's "Black and Yellow" playing from the room at the end of the hallway.

"That's my song! The party must be there," I say, letting the music lead me.

Tisha bangs loudly on the door twice, and the guy who

opens it gives us a dirty look that says he did not sign up to play doorman all night. I let out a shy, "Thanks" as we walk past him into the crowded living room area. After scanning the room and noticing that only a few other girls are in costume, I pull Tisha close to me.

"I'm gonna kick your ass, Tisha. I thought you said it was a costume party! Why are we the only ones dressed up?!"

Tisha gives me an apologetic look and shrugs her shoulders. "When I find Bernard, I'll ask him about it. Nobody will notice, though. It's crowded in here!"

I roll my eyes at her, as a guy in a 49ers jersey leans in. "You two must be freshmen or sophomores. The seniors pranked the lower class girls by telling them it was a costume party." He looks me up and down, licking his lips.

"You look cute, though."

"Yuck," I say, pulling Tisha away to the other side of the room.

"I can't believe Bernard would prank me!" Tisha whimpers, disappointment spread across her face.

"It's okay! We look good, and people will be too drunk to notice soon. Let's get a drink."

She nods, and I lead her over to the kitchen area. Bottles of Bacardi Dragonberry, Absolut Vodka, Hennessy, and Meyer's Rum are scattered across the kitchen counter. A large dispenser with a red liquid inside sits in the corner with the words "Jungle Juice" written on a piece of duct tape.

"Ooh, let's try that. I hope it's sweet," she says. Nothing like free liquor to put a girl in a better mood. I find two plastic red cups and place one under the opening of the dispenser, ready to fill our cups so we can get back to the party.

"You have to play with the knob a little bit to get it to pour."

I look up to see a guy with a caramel complexion, hazel

eyes, and shoulder-length locs watching me. I immediately focus on getting the juice out to distract me from noticing how cute he is.

"Thank you," I say, not bothering to give him eye contact.

"You're welcome...Ms. Kitty."

I hear the humor in Hazel-Eyed Cutie's voice and look up to see him smiling at me. He breaks into laughter once our eyes meet, and I start to take in his features. Clear, even skin tone. Long eyelashes. Very full lips. A dimple on the right cheek, but not on the left. I'm staring way too hard.

"That is *not* my name," I shoot back, smiling.

"Just out of curiosity, why are y'all in costumes?" he asks.

Tisha butts in between us. "A friend of mine said it was a costume party, but I see now that it was just a prank for the freshmen and sophomore girls to make us look like idiots."

"Some friend, huh?" he says to Tisha, still staring at me. "You two look nice, though. I like the tail," he says, winking at me. A guy standing next to him, who I'm assuming is a friend of his, nudges him and nods at Tisha.

Thank God I've finally gotten the dispenser to work so we can grab our drinks and get away from these guys.

"Well, thanks," I say. "And thanks for the tip."

"You're welcome, Ms. Kitty."

"I told you that's not my name."

"It's your name until you tell me your real name."

"I'm Melody. And you are?"

"Tyrell."

Tisha and Tyrell's friend introduce themselves, and my plan to bail is instantly shut down. I might as well make conversation. He can't be that bad, right?

"You go to school here? I've never seen you on campus before," I ask, curious to know who this guy is. Black students only make up 6% of USC's student population, so we pretty much all know of or have seen each other at least once in passing. Plus, I would've noticed someone this fine.

"I just transferred here from LACC. This is my first time really being on campus outside of just going to class."

"That's cool," I say, sipping my drink. "You stay on campus?"

"Nah, I'm commuting for now. I didn't apply for housing in time, but I'll be dorming next semester, so you can see me as much as you want."

"Who said I wanted to see you at all?"

"You wouldn't have asked if I go to school here if you didn't want to know."

"I was just curious, that's all. We don't have a lot of black faces on this campus."

"Yeah, I see that. You like it here so far?"

"I do," I say over the loud music. Tisha signals to me that she's done talking to Tyrell's friend, and that's my cue to wrap this conversation up. "Well, it was nice meeting you. We're gonna get back to the party now."

"That's cool."

I turn to walk away and feel a light tug on my arm.

"I don't want to wait until I get back on campus to talk to you again," Tyrell says to me, his mouth closer to my ear than a girl in a relationship should probably allow. "Can I get your number, Melody?"

"I'm sorry, I have a man," I whisper back in his ear.

"That's not what I asked you," he says, making us both laugh.

"I'll see you around, Tyrell."

"See you around, Kitty," he calls back.

I smile while I fight the urge to look over my shoulder as I walk away, because I know for sure he's watching me.

Tyrell - 2011
Sophomore Year

Melody walks away, and I can't help but admire her.

Dark chocolate-toned skin. Long, black hair that moves when she does. Pretty teeth with a smile that lingers. Big, beautiful brown eyes. And her body? Dangerous.

She said she had a man, but I don't see him anywhere.

G taps me on the shoulder, breaking my spell. We both transferred here from Los Angeles Community College, and this was our first party on campus. G heard some girls talking about it a few days ago and flirted his way into getting the details. His logic was simple: we needed to start being seen on campus if we wanted people to know who we were.

"Yo," he says, nodding in Melody's direction. "Wassup with that?"

"Ain't nothing," I shrug. "She said she got a man."

G chuckles. "When did that ever stop you?"

I laugh at the truth of his statement.

In the short year that I've known G, we've been everywhere together, from street basketball games to concerts to college parties. I've never shied away from talking to women I find attractive. When they tell me they have a man, I try twice. One, because I'm persistent, and two, because some like being chased and are looking for someone to go that extra mile. Sometimes it works, and sometimes I get rejected extra hard. I take it all on the chin.

Truthfully, I shouldn't be trying to talk to anyone at all since I have a girl I've been dealing with for a few months, Brittany. Brittany and I are not serious and really just mess around whenever we have time. Melody though...she's different. The kind of beauty I couldn't pass up.

"I'll try to get at her again," I say. "You know my rule. What's up with her friend?"

"Tisha. She's cool. Gave me her number and said she'd give me a tour of the campus."

I dap him up. G didn't use to talk to girls at all when I first met him. He always felt self-conscious about being short, but I told him that confidence is the most important part. The more we went out, the more I would try to encourage him to walk up to whoever he thought was attractive and try to strike up a conversation. Now? He's solid. He's a good wingman to have around.

"Let's go where the crowd is," I say.

I direct him to the living room, which is much more crowded now than it was 20 minutes ago when we arrived. It's amazing how many people can fit into a college dorm. Bodies everywhere. Music loud enough to rattle your chest. I spot Melody and Tisha in a corner dancing with two guys who look like this is their first time ever seeing two beautiful women up close.

The DJ transitions to the next song, and the entire place goes crazy.

"Cash Money Records taking over for the '99 and the 2000s..."

I don't hesitate. I make my way over to them, G following closely behind me. I give the dudes they were dancing with my best *get the fuck on* look, and they quickly exit.

Melody and Tisha are so busy throwing ass that they don't immediately notice us. That's my cue.

I get behind Melody and tug lightly on her tail, pulling her back so I can get closer to her. When she realizes it's me behind her, she glances back, confused at first—but she doesn't stop dancing. That's all I need.

We dance for the duration of the song, my hands settling at her waist. She grinds against me like she's making a point to show me exactly what I *won't* be getting later. Her body moves easy, confident, and controlled. I let my grip tighten just enough to let her know I'm there.

Once the tempo slows and she stands upright again, I lean in close.

"You could at least keep dancing with me," I say in her ear. "You already broke my heart earlier."

She laughs. "I'm only dancing with you because you can actually keep up. I'd rather you than dude you scared off."

"Oh, you saw that?" I grin. "I thought I was being low."

Melody turns to face me, eyes slowly dragging over me.

"You know what you look like," she says. "I'm sure you know that can be...intimidating."

I lick my lips at her, returning the once over she just gave to me.

"Do I intimidate you, Melody?"

The look she gives me says that she's more interested in me than I initially thought. And the feeling is damn sure mutual.

"Not at all, Tyrell," she says, with a cocky smile.

The crowd shifts, and she moves closer to me. Rihanna's *Rude Boy* comes on, and Melody backs into me again like it's instinct. She's a tease, but too fine for me to walk away from.

We spend most of the night like that. Dancing. Laughing. Moving with the group. But no matter where we are, Melody's eyes kept finding mine, and I can tell that if nothing else, she's attracted to me, and curious to know who I am and what I'm about.

Once the party ends, G and I walk the ladies to their dorms to make sure they're good. G and Tisha walk to the side to have their own private conversation. When they are out of earshot, Melody turns to face me.

"It was nice meeting you, Tyrell," she says. "You're a great dance partner."

I reach for her hand like I'm going to shake it, then pull her closer instead.

"It was nice to meet you as well, Ms. Kitty," I say. "I hope this isn't the last time I see you."

"I hope for your sake it isn't either."

Melody winks at me before she turns to walk away, and I smile and shake my head at her confidence, audacity, and sexiness.

I have a feeling I'll be seeing a lot more of her very soon.

Melody - 2011
Sophomore Year

I sn't it crazy how you can meet someone once and then suddenly see them everywhere you turn?

I've run into Tyrell twice since the party last weekend. Once, while Mike and I were walking arm in arm to class, and again when I walked past him in the library, sitting with a girl. Each time, we waved and smiled at each other like casual friends. We were both with people, which meant no awkward conversations and no lingering.

So imagine my surprise when I walked into the Thornton School of Music today and saw Tyrell sitting outside of the room I was supposed to be heading into in about 30 minutes.

He is dressed in black slacks, black dress shoes, and a black button-down shirt, holding a stack of papers, intensely focused. Calm. Fine.

Is he auditioning, too? I wonder.

He notices me as I get closer and immediately breaks into a smile.

"Wassup, Kitty? What you doing here all dressed up?"

I glance down at myself, neatly dressed in a long-sleeved, off-the-shoulder dress and matching heels.

"I told you my name," I say. "And you still insist on calling me that."

"I like Kitty better," he says in a flirty way.

"You are too much! Are you here for the audition?"

At USC, you had to audition in your sophomore year to take any of the minors offered by the Thornton School of Music. I was here to audition for Musical studies, concentrating in vocal arts.

"Yeah, I'm auditioning for the Jazz studies minor."

"Oh, that's amazing! I'm doing Musical studies for vocal. What instrument?"

"Guess."

I look at his hands. Soft on the outside, but rough on the inside when you really looked. Just like my uncle's hands. A pianist's hands.

"Definitely piano."

Tyrell looks surprised. "How did you know?"

"My uncle plays. His hands look the same way."

He chuckles. "So, you sing, huh? Why not just major in vocal instead of the minor?"

"I wanted to," I admit. "But with the recession from a few years ago, I was too worried about getting a job. You know it can be hard for musicians. I figured a minor was my safest bet." I shrug. "I should be asking you the same."

"Same reason," he says. "Eventually, I'd like to do music full-time, but my family doesn't come from money, and I need job security. I'm a Finance major."

"I hear that. How long have you been playing?"

"I started playing when I was young, like around five or six.

My grandmother had a piano and first taught me to play gospel songs. I started playing in my school band in middle school and just stayed with it. After my mom passed a few years ago, I started playing more heavily to help me cope." He pauses. "People told me I was really good at it, so...here I am."

"I'm sorry to hear that," I say softly. "I'm sure your mom is really proud of you for continuing to play."

"Thanks. Yeah, I hope so." He looks at me for a moment. "I can't imagine not playing. How long have you been singing?"

I hear it then. The familiar edge of grief in his voice.

"Since I was eight," I say. "After my dad passed, my uncle played the piano a lot. I used to watch him all the time. One day, he asked me to sit with him at the piano and started teaching me a Chaka Khan song to sing. I sang a few notes, and he put me in vocal lessons the next week."

"You must be really good," he says. "And I'm sorry to hear about your dad. I'm sure singing made you feel a lot better at the time."

"You know what's funny?" I begin, "My dad and uncle were identical twins. When my dad passed, my uncle stepped up and raised me. I missed my dad deeply, of course, but it almost felt like he was there the whole time through my uncle." I shake my head. "Sorry, that probably sounds weird."

I'm oversharing. For some reason, I feel comfortable talking to Tyrell about this, even though I barely know him.

"No, it's not weird at all," he says quickly, smiling in a way that puts me at ease. "I'm glad you told me that. It's good to talk to somebody who understands what I've been through."

He pats my hand in a friendly way, and I can't help but smile back at him.

"Melody Ford?"

A woman steps out of the audition room, clipboard in hand. *It's time.*

"Yes, I'm here," I say, standing and gathering my things.

I came here a little earlier to prepare for my audition, but got caught up in conversation with Tyrell. I didn't realize how nervous I actually was until my name was called. The nervousness must be written on my face, because Tyrell taps my arm as I'm about to walk away.

"Hey," he says. "Don't be nervous. You got this. Make your dad proud."

I smile and nod at him. "Thank you."

"Good luck, Kitty."

I roll my eyes, smiling, and walk into the room. *Here goes nothing.*

In the audition room, I introduce myself to three faculty members seated behind a long table. All are dressed in business casual and wearing stern, intimidating looks.

"Ms. Ford," one asks, "what do you hope to accomplish with a minor in Musical studies?"

"I want to expand my range and develop the skills I need to launch my career as an R&B singer."

The faculty all look at each other.

"Are you aware," another asks, "that our vocal studies curriculum focuses heavily on the study of classical and opera music?"

They already don't think I belong here, but I don't let the question defeat me.

"Yes," I say. "And as an R&B artist, I draw references from all genres and music styles. Some of the greats, like Mariah

Carey and Minnie Ripperton, were classically trained, and it shows in their music."

"Very well then," he nods, seemingly pleased with my response. "Please present the title of your piece and sheet music for our accompanist."

"I'll be singing 'Home' performed by Stephanie Mills from *The Wiz.*"

The accompanist nods as I hand him my sheet music and whisper a few notes about key changes.

The nervousness that I felt before I walked into the room has been replaced by my need to nail this audition and prove that I deserve to be here. As the accompanist plays the introduction, I focus on letting the lyrics of the song overtake me, and start singing like I've practiced so many times before. Once I've let out my last note, the accompanist smiles at me, and I know I've nailed it.

I thank him quietly and turn back to the panel. Their faces were stoic during my song, but they are whispering amongst themselves, looking back and forth between me and their list.

"Ms. Ford," a woman says, "thank you for auditioning. You have undeniable talent, and we'd like to welcome you—unofficially—to the Thornton School of Music. Congratulations."

I nearly jump up and down from my excitement. A squeal escapes me, and I thank the panel profusely as they clap. I shake each of their hands as they introduce themselves to me. I walk out of the room with all of the confidence in the world, ready to tell Tyrell how well the audition went.

You just nailed your audition, and the first person you want to tell is a stranger you've barely had two conversations with? I question myself.

Before I can overthink it, the same woman with the clipboard from earlier calls out,

"Tyrell Hampton?"

Tyrell gathers his materials and stands up, walking past me as I exit the audition room.

"Good luck," I whisper.

"Thank you," he says, with no sign of nervousness on his face. There is only pure confidence.

After little debate, I decide that I'm going to wait for Tyrell to finish his audition. The rooms are soundproof, so I can't hear anything that's going on inside. I twiddle my thumbs for what feels like an eternity when I hear the door crack open. When he comes out smiling, relief hits me harder than I expect.

"You waited," he says, happiness exuding from his face.

"I wanted to know how it went for you."

"I got in!" he exclaims, and I laugh at his excitement.

"Me too!"

"Congrats to us," he says, giving me an unexpected hug. *I didn't notice how good he smelled before.* "We should celebrate."

"I don't know if that's a good idea," I quickly state, smoothing out my dress as I release myself from his embrace.

"It'll be quick. What—you scared your punk-ass man might catch us out?"

Tyrell scoffs as he gathers his items, then nods his head in the direction of the exit of the building, encouraging me to follow him. Running on pure adrenaline and the excitement of my acceptance, I ignore the fact that this is actually a bad idea and follow him anyway.

In the student parking lot, he opens the passenger side door of his Jeep, guiding me in.

"Tyrell, where are you taking me?"

"I'm taking you to celebrate," he says. "Don't worry, I'll bring you back to your man soon and in one piece."

"I would appreciate that, thank you," I fire back, sarcastically.

"You and this dude really serious?"

Tyrell's expression changes to one that resembles curiosity, and I decide to be careful with my words. If I say the wrong thing, he might think he has a chance. If he didn't have a chance, though, I wouldn't be in the car with him right now. I quickly snap out of the ridiculousness of that last thought, responding,

"We are *very* serious. He loves me, and I love him. He even said he wants to get married once we graduate. So yes, this is very real, and you can stop trying to get with me now."

I roll my eyes at Tyrell, a smirk imprinted on my face.

"And you believe him?"

"He hasn't given me a reason not to."

He nods, respecting it. I get the impression that maybe this is the last time he'll bring this up. Although I barely know the guy, he doesn't strike me as the type who's thirsty and will continue to pursue someone who isn't giving him the time of day.

"I'll leave you alone, then. But we can be cool, right? I know we're going to have some of the same classes together, and it would be nice to have a friend who's in the same program as me."

I am quiet for a few seconds as we turn into the parking lot of Emerald's Bakery. If there's one thing I can't resist, it's a baked good. Sweets always put me in a good mood, and the treats from this bakery were some of my favorites in LA.

"That's cool," I say. "Not like you'd get the chance to be more than that, anyway."

We both laugh, and Tyrell counters, "Trust me, I know

how to be patient. I'll wear you down one day when you least expect it."

"I wouldn't count on it."

We smile at each other as we exit the car and walk into the bakery, welcoming the start of a friendship unlike anything either of us would ever experience again.

It's seventy-four degrees in LA on a Saturday evening, and I'm home for the first time in weeks. Between rehearsals for our upcoming performance on Anderson West and working on new music, Mel and I have been all business lately. I've gotten used to it, especially since our song "Tonight" went viral on TikTok last year and jump-started our music career. With a viral song came an influx of opportunities within the music industry. Suddenly, everything moved fast.

Too fast.

Balancing my corporate job as a financial analyst with music became damn near impossible. It wasn't any easier for Melody, trying to juggle her role as a high school social worker while building momentum as an artist. After years of talking about starting our own R&B group since back in college, we finally decided to bet on ourselves, trust our talent, and leave our careers behind to pursue music full-time.

Since then, it has definitely been challenging trying to keep a normal social life. Neither one of us has been able to hang out with friends, and I haven't seen Natalie—the woman I'm dating—in weeks.

Despite how exhausted I feel, you'd think I'd enjoy being in my spot right now. A $7,000-a-month apartment with a view I barely get to look at. Time to rest. Time to breathe.

But instead of catching up on rest, all I want tonight is good company.

I consider calling Natalie.

...No.

She's cool, don't get me wrong, and the sex is good enough. She's easy to be around in small doses. But there's nothing there. No pull. No spark. And the more honest I am with myself, the clearer it becomes.

On Valentine's Day, I went all out trying to see if that spark could be forced. I paid a decorator to line my apartment with rose petals, fill the place with balloons, dozens of arranged vases of roses, gifts—the whole nine yards. At that point, we had been dating for a few months, and I told myself that I needed to put in some real effort. I thought maybe if I focused all of my efforts on her, at least for the day, I would feel the spark that I thought was missing between us.

That might've been the dumbest plan I've ever come up with.

By most people's standards, we had the most romantic Valentine's Day. The mood was right. We said all of the right things. We did all of the right things.

Still, the passion was missing.

I like Natalie as a person, but when I'm with her, I don't feel like I can be myself. There is no joking. No banter. No talking about anything and everything that comes to mind. Our conversations seem so...formal. And now that I think about it, the only time she loosens up is when I'm inside of her.

This realization alone affirms that I won't be calling her tonight.

Instead, I call Mel.

We've been close friends for so long that formalities are out of the window with us. Because of our schedule, I'm sure she's equally as worn out and probably at home. I dial her up, finally getting her on the fourth ring.

"Hi, Sweetie!" she answers, cheerful as always.

"Hey, Kitty. What you up to?"

"Not much, just home right now and cooking a little dinner. What's up with you?"

"Ooo, I called at the right time," I say. "You made enough for me?"

"How do you know I don't have company?"

"You wouldn't have picked up the phone if you were that busy," I laugh. "And besides that, nobody wants to deal with your mean ass."

For as long as I've known Melody, she's always been no-nonsense with men. They only get one time to fuck up, and they're gone. Sometimes, it's not even a fuck up. She once cut a dude off because he pronounced the *L* in salmon and had a receding hairline.

"You know damn well that's not true," she says, softening her voice. "I'm an absolute angel."

We both laugh.

"Bring your greedy ass on if you want," she says. "I'll be around."

"Bet. I'll be there in thirty."

We hang up, and I grab my keys and wallet.

Being around someone I don't have to perform for—someone I can just be myself with—is exactly what I need tonight.

CHAPTER 2

Tyrell

Mel lives in one of the high rises on the corner of 4th Street and Main. For as long as she's been an adult with a real job, she's lived in this apartment. She and our homegirl, Tisha, scored a great deal on a two-bedroom here shortly after the building first went up. About five years ago, Tisha met her now-husband, Darnell, and moved out into a house in Sherman Oaks. Mel kept the place, converted Tisha's old bedroom into an office-slash-closet, and made it her own.

I've spent a lot of time in this apartment over the years.

Back in our early-mid twenties, Mel and Tisha used to host game nights and karaoke nights regularly. As many noise complaints as they received from neighbors fed up with our loud, drunken nights, I'm honestly surprised they were able to even keep the apartment for as long as they did.

On my drive over, the memory of the surprise party they threw me at the apartment when I turned twenty-eight comes to mind, and I can't help but smile.

Tisha called me earlier that day in a frenzy, saying something about a leak under their sink that was supposedly getting worse by the minute. Since it was a weekend, the management company wouldn't do anything about it until Monday morning. I rushed over there dressed in sweats and a t-shirt, toolkit in hand, only to walk into a living room full of twenty of my friends from college and work screaming, "Surprise!"

I remember how annoyed I felt at being so underdressed for my own party—and relieved that I didn't have to actually fix anything.

After playing multiple rounds of Kings and Taboo and taking every shot handed to me, I got so drunk that I passed out on their couch in nothing but the shorts under my sweatpants. I woke up covered in a pink blanket with a pink bonnet covering my locs, Mel's doing, of course.

I've made a lot of great memories with the people I met when I was nineteen and just trying to figure life out. Some of the fondest ones happened in a 900 sq. ft. bachelorette pad in the middle of Studio City.

Life has definitely shifted since then.

It's crazy to think the community that we built when everyone lived a five-minute walk across campus now looks so different. Careers. Families. Responsibilities. Out of our original friend group of twelve, only seven of us still reside in LA. Getting together these days is few and far between. I'm always grateful to see my people doing well and advancing, but I do wish we got together more often.

Even Mel and I don't really *hang out* anymore. We work together, but we hardly see each other for things other than work. Now that I think about it, I can't even remember the last time the two of us just sat around to talk about something other than a song we were writing, an upcoming appearance, or a business meeting.

Tonight, though, I'm not talking about work. I just want to hang out with someone who really knows me.

I park in the guest parking area and grab the bottle of Caymus wine from the backseat. Even though we're close friends and technically co-workers, I don't believe in showing up to anyone's house empty-handed, especially after I invited myself over. Upstairs, I give a rhythmic knock to signal that it's me. I've been using the same knock since college days, when I would stop by Mel and Tisha's dorm to chill and eat up their snacks, or to borrow an ID for their meal plan because I ran out of money on mine.

It's an unspoken familiarity between us.

Mel opens the door wearing an athleisure set, hair pulled back into a low bun. She has the kind of natural beauty people often praise women from the 90s for.

"Hey, Sweetie!" She greets me with her high-pitched voice and a smile.

"Hey, Kitty." I lean in for a hug, returning her same warm energy. She pulls away after our embrace and gives me a once over.

"You look nice! Got a hot date after this?"

She loves questioning me about things that aren't her business.

"Thank you. I wish I could say the same for you," I smirk, which earns me a shove. "No, I don't have a date, I just felt like looking decent and getting out of the house. As drained as I am from all the shit we've been doing the last few weeks, for some reason, I'm not in the mood to be home."

"Understandable," she says. "It's been a hectic few weeks. I'm grateful for it, but tired. I was actually thinking of taking some time off soon."

Mel is a workaholic, so to hear her talk about a vacation immediately throws me off.

"Is everything okay?" I ask. "You've never once mentioned needing time off."

She gives me a look that tells me I might've pushed too far, and she doesn't want to talk about this, so I try to lighten the mood.

"Or is being around my sexy all the time just too much for you to handle?"

"Tyrell, please," she laughs. "I just want to give myself a chance to relax before our schedule gets to be too crazy. I don't want to burn myself out—and you shouldn't either."

I consider her words as she fixes my plate.

Between lead vocals, press, features for other artists, an undeniable star quality, and her outgoing personality, Mel carries more of the spotlight. I prefer to take more of a background role. Production. Arranging. Adding vocals when they're needed. Letting the work speak for itself. So far, this balance has worked pretty well for us.

We sit at her dining table, eating and talking about work. I didn't come here to talk about our upcoming schedule at all, but I can tell Mel needed to vent to someone who actually understands how she might be feeling. The music business is tricky to navigate, and although our friends and family are supportive, they have no idea about its inner workings.

I finish up my food and push my plate aside.

"Let's go out for drinks. Take our minds off all this."

She smiles. "You're treating. Let me get ready."

"Melody, when do you ever pay for anything around me?"

I don't believe in women paying for anything in my presence. It's one of the first lessons my grandmother taught me when I was a teenager trying to figure out dating and girls for the first time. She used to say, "A lady should never be with you and have to go in her purse."

"Hey, I took you out for your birthday last year!" she says.

"Would've done it this year too if you weren't busy with Natasha."

She says this in such a matter-of-fact way, then smirks at me as she clears off the table. She's setting a trap for me to correct her and tell her what's going on between Natalie and me. I don't take the bait. I've been very quiet about how dating is going—and I'd like to keep it that way.

"Her name is Natalie," I correct. "And you know it's hard for me to celebrate my birthday on that day. Women don't care if it's my birthday; they want to be wined and dined on Valentine's Day."

"The right woman would make sure you're celebrated," she says. "I'll be back in twenty minutes."

I don't admit to her that she's right.

Melody walks back into the living room twenty minutes later, as promised, dressed and ready to go. She is wearing her hair up in one of those messy kinds of buns with pieces framing her face. The form fitting black pants that flare out, paired with her top that is low cut and slightly cropped, with a lacy sweater over it, make her look like Maia Campbell from that sitcom, "In the House."

"How do I look?" she asks, spinning to give me a full 360.

Mel is a beautiful woman, and I'd be lying if I didn't acknowledge that. Between her deep, chocolate skin that always looks like the sun itself came down from the sky to kiss it, her big brown eyes that feel like they're looking through you, her full lips that accompany a wide smile with the most perfect teeth, and her figure-8 body that she works on at the gym 5 days a week, she *is* the beauty standard. I've always found her to be incredibly attractive, even when we were nineteen and she hadn't yet developed her grown woman body. Once we established that we were only going to be friends, though, I never verbally gave her much feedback about the way she looked, and I don't plan to start.

"Better than you did 20 minutes ago," I reply with a teasing grin. "Let's get out of here."

CHAPTER 3

Tyrell

We decide on a dive bar not too far from Mel's apartment. When we walk in, it's starting to get crowded, but not to a point where we're uncomfortable. I spot two empty bar stools and motion for Mel to follow me over, grabbing her hand as I maneuver us through the crowd. I pull out a stool for her and hang her bag on one of the hooks beneath the bar counter.

"Hey, folks!" says a blonde bartender, multi-tasking as she clears away glasses and wipes down the counter. "What can I get for you?"

"Mel?" I ask.

"Um...can you make me something sweet?" she says.

We seem to have the same conversation every time we go out. Mel is one of the few women I know in their thirties that doesn't have a signature drink. She just wants something "sweet and strong."

Much like herself.

"I'll have an old fashioned, please," I say. "Thank you."

The bartender hurries off to make our drinks, and I turn to tease Mel for her drink choice. Before I can get a word out, I'm interrupted by an enthusiastic voice coming from a nearby microphone.

"Hey folks! We're starting karaoke in about twenty minutes. Meet me here on the stage if you'd like to sign up!"

Mel's face lights up immediately.

"*No*," I say as sternly as I can muster.

"Come onnnn," she whines. "We have to! It'll be fun."

She is too excited for this, which doesn't surprise me. Mel wouldn't miss an opportunity to perform. She'd sing to a brick wall if she thought it might be entertained by her.

"Why don't *you* go up there and sing something," I suggest. "I'll sit here and be moral support."

She hops off of her bar stool before I finish my sentence.

"You owe me for entertaining you tonight," she says, leaning in to kiss my cheek before walking off.

I watch her make her way to the front, giggling with the employee holding the sign-up sheet. We are the only Black people in the bar, but Mel doesn't let that deter her. She never lets anything stop her from doing what she wants to do, and it's one of the qualities I admire most about her.

She comes back practically bouncing from excitement.

"I think I'm first up," she says, sipping her fruity drink. "I'm actually a little nervous."

"You?! Nervous?" I laugh. "We've been on stages way bigger than this."

"Yeah, but intimate crowds are more intimidating to me," she says. "You're closer to your audience, and you can feel more of their response. If they're not feeling me, I'll know immediately."

At this, her face grimaces.

"You're taking this way too seriously," I tell her. "Besides, most of the people in here are already drunk. They don't know us, and they probably can't even sing. There are no A&Rs here, Mel."

"First up for karaoke," the employee announces on the mic. "Melody! Melody, you're on!"

She takes a long swig of her drink and sashays to the stage, looking back at me with uncertainty written all over her face.

I wave her off and mouth, "You'll be fine."

A few people clap politely as she grabs the mic.

"Hi, my name is Melody, and I'm going to sing '*Something to Talk About*' by Bonnie Raitt."

I laugh quietly. She knows about three country songs, and this is one of her favorites. She chose something familiar—classic Mel, always thinking about the crowd.

More people applaud this time. As soon as the music starts, she sways her hips along with the beat, and the energy shifts.

She starts to sing, and people are instantly tuned in. Conversations trail off. Heads turn. People pay attention.

I'd be lying if I said she wasn't doing a great job.

Aside from her superior singing abilities, she knows how to work a crowd. She's giving eye contact to the men ogling her, and inviting the crowd to sing with her by holding the mic out. By the second chorus, the whole bar is on their feet, singing and clapping along.

She looks at me and winks.

For a second, I forget we're just friends.

A couple next to me seemingly witnesses this interaction.

"Your girlfriend's awesome!" the guy says.

"Oh," I laugh awkwardly. "She's not my girlfriend. We're just friends."

His wife leans across him. "I don't think so after tonight. You see the way she looks at you?! You'd be a fool not to get with her."

"Yeah," the husband cuts in. "She's hot!"

His wife shoots him a look and elbows him, causing us all to laugh. I take a sip of my drink as Mel finishes up to the sound of the audience erupting in applause.

When she comes offstage, people stop to high-five and compliment her. She speaks to everyone who stops her and thanks them for their kind words. Men offer her drinks and shots, which she declines, pointing in my direction. I wave at the men, who quickly back off, as I assume they decided that having to deal with me isn't worth the trouble.

Mel skips over to me, all smiles.

"How did I do?! Could you tell I was nervous?"

"You were amazing!" I say. "You didn't look nervous at all."

"Aww, thanks. And you're welcome for the entertainment. You owe me."

"I'll buy you a drink for your efforts. Another fruity one?"

"No," she says. "Let's do a shot."

"Oh, you on *that* type of time tonight," I laugh. "Shit, let's do it then."

The couple from a few minutes ago overhears our conversation, and the husband calls out to the bartender.

"Can we get four shots over here? Johnnie Walker good with y'all?" he asks, as he turns to Mel and I.

I extend my hand to him. "Thanks, man. Tyrell. This is Melody."

Melody extends her hand to shake his and his wife's hand, and they are eager to chat her up about how long she's been singing. After we toast and take our shots, the couple circles back.

"So, Melody," the wife starts. "Tyrell says you two are just friends. I find that hard to believe."

Mel smiles—the polite, media-trained smile she uses when she's uncomfortable.

"Yeah, we've been friends since college. We go way back."

Before the couple can push further, I shift the conversation back to them.

"So, how long have you two been married?" I ask, in my most inquisitive sounding voice. If there's one thing I know about couples that are overly social and on the verge of being drunk, it's that they don't turn down the opportunity to talk about their relationship. Turns out my theory is true, and Mel and I spend the next fifteen minutes engulfed in a conversation with the couple about their wedding, and "truths" about married life.

My phone in my pocket buzzes, and I see a text from my boy G in our group chat.

G

Heading to that new spot Dirty On 85 in 30 with Kev. Pull up if y'all around.

I lean toward Mel, using this as an opportunity to bail from our current conversation.

"You wanna meet up with G and Kev?"

Mel's face oozes with relief.

"We're going to head out to meet up with some friends," she tells the couple. "It was so nice meeting you two."

"Nice to meet you two as well," the wife says.

She leans into Mel, and I hear her poor attempt at a hushed voice. "Honey, don't ignore what's right in front of you. He's obviously into you. Give him a chance!"

Mel smiles earnestly and replies just as loudly, "I'll think about it."

Outside of the bar, she exhales.

"Thanks for the save back there."

"What kind of fake boyfriend would I be if I didn't save you from awkward moments?"

She stops walking to stare at me for a few seconds, giving me a look that I can't recognize.

"What?" I ask. "Why are you staring at me like that?"

"Nothing," she says after a second. "Just...nevermind."

She links her arm in mine as we make our way to the next spot.

"Let's go."

I don't know if it was the adrenaline from singing, or the shot we took earlier creeping up on me, but the wife's words from the bar won't leave my head.

He's obviously into you.

Tyrell and I have an evident natural flow between us, so I can see why people would think we're together. I was, however, a little thrown off by her certainty.

What is she seeing that I'm not?

And maybe even more concerning: why am I not completely repulsed by that thought?

Those thoughts stay with me as we head into *Dirty on 85*, a new lounge opened by two brothers from Atlanta. I do my best to shake them loose, telling myself that I'm reading too much into a drunk stranger's commentary. I always do this. Overthink. Rewind conversations. Assign meaning where there might be none.

Ty and I spot our friends right away. G, Kev, Kim, and Sydney are already settled in, drinks in hand. I give a hug to the guys first, and when I reach to greet Kim and Sydney, I notice their eyes floating back and forth between Tyrell and me.

"Hey girl!" Kim chimes, kissing me on the cheek. "Why do you and Ty look like y'all were on a date?"

"Girl, please!" I counter, waving her off. "We were just at a bar grabbing drinks. You forgot we work together?"

"Since when did that ever stop anyone?" Sydney asks. "Y'all look like y'all have other plans, and we're keeping you from them."

"Syd!" I shriek, laughing at her brashness. "You both need to chill. We've been all work the last month or two, and just decided to hang out to take our minds off the busy schedule. Nothing more, nothing less."

"Mmmmhmmm," Kim says, rolling her eyes. "That's how it always starts."

I pretend not to hear that last comment.

The guys have secured a section, bottles of Ace of Spades and 1942 on the table. R&B and Hip-Hop blasts through the speakers, and for a while, it feels like college again. We dance, laugh, sing, and record every funny moment on our phones.

Except, something is different.

Tyrell keeps looking at me.

Not casually. Not the way he usually does. It's more focused. More intentional. Kim and Syd take turns playfully dancing with all of the guys, but I stick to G and Kev. Normally, Ty and I act as unofficial dance partners. Tonight, we both seem to be avoiding physical contact, yet can't keep our eyes off of one another.

It feels...loaded.

G suggests we all take a shot. I down mine, let the burn settle, then make a decision. The tension is starting to feel heavier than it should.

I walk over to Ty.

"Why haven't you danced with me?" I immediately ask as he turns around.

"Why haven't *you* danced with me?" he raises an eyebrow. "You're the one in the corner avoiding me like the plague. Did I do something wrong?"

"No," I say quickly. "My mind was elsewhere. I'm sorry."

"It's cool," he says, smiling. "I know my sexiness can be overwhelming."

"Boy, shut up."

I nudge his shoulder, expecting him to laugh it off. Instead, he pulls me into him just as the DJ transitions into a mid-tempo Afrobeats track. Our friends pair off around us, and suddenly, it's like there's only the two of us.

We start dancing with space between us, bodies barely touching. Seconds later, his hand settles at my waist. Firm. Confident. He pulls me closer, and before I can think too much about it, I'm leaning against his chiseled chest, his body moving easily with mine as I whine my hips to the rhythm.

"You smell good," he breathes softly into my ear.

The deepness of his voice immediately heats up my skin in a way I am completely unprepared for.

I turn to face him, needing to see his expression. The look in his eyes is sincere, yet beckoning. I feel more drawn to him in this moment than I care to admit.

"Ty," I say quietly. "What's going on?"

"You tell me," he replies. "I'm just dancing."

"You know what I'm talking about," I say, sharper than I intend.

"I don't, because you're not being clear."

As we stare at each other, I observe the details of his face, my eyes drifting down to his full lips. I find myself wondering how they'd feel against mine before I can stop myself.

Ty leans in, close enough that my breath catches. For a split second, I think he's going to kiss me. Instead, his mouth brushes my ear.

"Is there something you want me to know, Melody?" he asks.

The huskiness of his voice instantly softens mine.

"Tyrell," I say, forcing myself to stay grounded. "What do you want from me?"

I need to hear it out loud. I need to know that the energy I'm feeling isn't just in my head, and I'm not misinterpreting the last two hours of our interactions. Tyrell is...flirting with me. And...I think I like it.

"I think we both know the answer to that," he declares.

Then, he pulls back, winks at me, and walks away, leaving me standing there speechless with a smile I can't help but show.

And thinking far too much for my own good.

Melody and I dance for a few more songs, and with each one, I pull her a little closer. It isn't unusual for us to dance together, or for her to occasionally twerk on me. We've always been this way with each other.

Tonight feels different.

I can't take my eyes off of her, and I don't want to be away from her for too long. My attraction to her has skyrocketed in what seems like a matter of minutes, and I don't quite understand how I even got to this point. Was it the liquor? Or is it that she seems so relaxed around me, and how relaxed I am around her?

I think about how I couldn't keep my eyes off of her when she was singing earlier. How even strangers noticed something between us just by the way she looked at me. How, even in a crowd filled with beautiful women, she's the only one I'm drawn to. How, just moments ago, I had to stop myself from kissing her.

As the current song ends, I shake off the possibility of what all of these feelings might mean, and pull away from Melody, just as our friends decide they want to leave the lounge to get some food.

We end up at a diner, eating breakfast food, laughing, and joking all night. Even though we don't see each other often anymore, nights like this remind me that we haven't missed a thing. We joke about our past and present lives, and for the first time in a while, my mind feels quiet. Free.

At the end of the night, we say our goodbyes, and I accompany Melody, who is visibly drunk at this point, back to her apartment to get my car, ensure her safety and lowkey, gauge what she's feeling.

As soon as we settle in the backseat of the black truck, Melody stretches her legs out, conveniently landing them in my lap. She starts removing clips and pins from her hair, fluffing it down until her loose curls frame her face. She looks incredibly...sexy. She closes her eyes, and I immediately laugh at her.

"You had a good time tonight, huh?"

"I did!" she responds, giggling a little bit too much for the question. "It was so much fun! I love being around you guys. My feet are killing me, though."

I glance down at her feet, still resting in my lap, tangled in her strappy heels. Without thinking too hard about it, I start untying them.

"What are you doing?" she asks, sounding more amused than hesitant.

"I don't want to hear you complain about your feet for the whole thirty minute ride back to your place," I say. "I gotta do my part."

I cradle one of her feet in my hands and start massaging it. I know I'm pushing it. I also know this is the only excuse I can use to touch her before the night ends.

Melody tilts her head back, closing her eyes.

"I never knew you were so good with your hands."

"You have no idea."

The words slip out louder than I mean to. We freeze, staring at each other. The same look we shared when she was singing. The same one on the dance floor. Curiosity and lust now linger in both of our eyes.

I break our silence.

"Mel, I—"

"Wait. Excuse me, Sir," she says to the driver. "Can you turn the volume up? This is my song!"

The driver turns the volume up, and Tony! Toni! Toné!'s *(Lay Your Head On My) Pillow* blares from the car's sound system.

Mel starts singing, and I sing along, not taking my eyes off her.

"This is one of my favorite songs," she says, pure contentment in her voice.

"Yeah? Well," I reply quietly, "this song is for you, then."

We spend the rest of the ride singing along to whatever 90s R&B playlist the driver has going. I keep massaging Mel's feet, occasionally tickling the bottom just to hear her laugh uncontrollably. By the time we arrive at her building, the moment feels suspended, like neither of us wants it to end.

I re-tie the straps of her shoes and thank the driver.

"I don't need help getting upstairs, Ty. I'm good," she says, wobbling a few steps. We both laugh.

As we begin to walk, she loops her arm through mine, and I pull her closer to me.

Once we're off the elevator and in front of her door, I reach into her purse for her keys, open her door, and guide her inside. She immediately makes her way to her plush green couch, plopping down and dropping her bag next to her. I sit down too, pick up her legs, and start untying her shoes again.

She exhales deeply.

"Thank you," she sighs, giving me that same look from earlier.

"For what?" I ask.

"For being a gentleman. For taking care of me. And for showing me a good time. I needed it."

"I know you did," I say. "And I needed it, too. I'm glad I decided to stop by."

"I'm glad you did, too."

She looks at me like she's glad for more than just the night out, and that's my cue to leave before I cross a line I won't be able to walk back from.

"Well, let me get outta here," I say, rising from the couch. "You sure you're good?"

"I'm sure! Thank you, though," she says, standing to walk me to the door.

"Goodnight, Mel."

"Goodnight, Sweetie."

She rises on her toes and presses a soft kiss to my cheek. We smile at each other until I gesture for her to close her door.

"And make sure you lock it, drunk ass," I tease.

I hear her giggling on the other side of the door as the locks click, and shake my head on the way to the elevator.

During the ride back to my apartment, I replay the night. Why was I all of a sudden so entranced by this woman? Mel and I have had our share of fun nights out, but I've never felt like this at the end of them. Something shifted between us tonight. Something that makes me feel like what I've been missing has been right in front of me this whole time.

I reach for my phone, ready to ask her if she wants to meet up for coffee the next day and talk. Before I even unlock the screen, a series of texts pop up with her name displayed.

I smile at the influx of texts from her inebriated brain, then frown at her reminder.

Just friends.

Mel's right. We are *just* friends, and that's probably for the best. I send her a simple text, leaning my head back and closing my eyes.

What a night.

CHAPTER 6

Tyrell

May 2014
Senior Year

"Mel! Open up!"

My voice is as loud as socially acceptable during this time of night, as I knock on the door of Melody's apartment. My final for Jazz Ensemble is due in twelve hours, and Mel is the only one I trust outside of my professors to give me real, honest feedback.

After we met during the fall of our sophomore year, Mel and I bonded quickly. Music did that. So did grief. Losing our parents gave us an unspoken understanding, and somehow our personalities—oil and vinegar—still meshed well. Seeing each other constantly through the music department made it easy to become fast friends, and before long, our friend groups blended into one. Now, I see Mel almost every day. Being around her and our homegirl Tisha has become my normal.

The door finally opens. Mel stands there sleepy-eyed, hair pulled back into a messy bun, wearing a USC T-shirt, shorts,

43

and fuzzy slippers. She looks like she was deep into her fourth dream before I interrupted.

"Ty, why are you banging on my door like that?" she asks. "This better not be about that final, because we already went over it twice this week and I told you it was perfect."

"Hello to you too!" I chirp. "I changed some things, and I need your help."

I lean in to kiss her cheek. She rolls her eyes but steps aside, letting me in. Their dorm room is one of the nicest on campus, and I head straight for my keyboard in the living room. I'm here so much that I got tired of dragging my keyboard around every time I had an idea that I had to run by Melody, so I saved up and bought a second one just to keep here.

I sit on the bench and retrieve the sheet music from my backpack.

"I keep telling you to stop coming by here unannounced, Ty. Your keyboard being here is already a cock block."

She sits down on the couch across from me, glasses now on, ready to play reviewer and producer.

"Please. Everybody knows we're just friends," I reply. "If you can't get a man up in here, that's your fault."

"Whatever," she says, waving me off. "Lucky for you, I'm too tired to go back and forth. Now let me hear it so you can get the fuck out."

"Don't do me like that, Mel," I say. "You know you're the only one I trust with this. My classmates are straight haters. They'll steal my ideas in a minute."

She sighs. "Okay, okay. Let me hear it."

She sits up now, showing more interest. I begin to play my piece, pointing out the changes I made. She closes her eyes and listens, allowing me to play the entire piece without interrupting. When I finish, she opens them. A big smile spreads across her face, showing off the deep dimples embedded in her cheeks.

"So?" I ask, anxious about her feedback.

"I love it!" she says. "I didn't think it could get any more perfect, but those changes really took it to another level. Oh! That reminds me—I wrote something yesterday that I think would go well with the melodies you wrote."

Before I can respond, Mel is already rushing to her bedroom, where I'm sure she's getting the pink notebook that she writes all of her songs in.

"You don't think I should change anything else?" I call after her.

"If you change one more thing, I'm kicking you out," she yells back. "*No*! It's perfect the way it is."

I won't lie, I immediately feel better after hearing that. Although Mel doesn't play any instruments, she has an incredible ear for music and can pick up on chord changes and progressions better than most musicians I know.

"Thank you," I say, exhaling. "This shit is stressing me out. You know I'm hard on myself."

"You're such a perfectionist," she replies. "But I tell you all the time—you're a genius when it comes to this. One day, you'll finally see what I've been seeing for years."

I take in her words, which I value more than I let her know. I don't trust very many people with my art, often holding the songs I create near to me. Her words affirm me, and I hate to admit that I look to her opinions for validation.

"Thank you for saying that, Mel," I say quietly. "You know this all gets to me."

"I don't know why," she laughs. "You're the most talented person I know. Anyone who knows you knows that. I don't know why you can't see it for yourself."

She reaches over and rests her hand on my thigh, gently patting it as she whispers, "Trust yourself more."

"Do you trust me?"

I don't know where the fuck that came from, but I can't take it back now. Mel and I are both staring at each other. Her big, brown eyes search mine like she's trying to see my soul.

"With my life," is all she says.

We sit in silence for a moment.

Everything that I've wanted with Brittany—and every other woman I've dealt with in the last three years—Mel gives me without trying. She believes in me. She supports my art. She understands the sacrifice and my dedication to my craft. Outside of my grandmother, she's one of the few women who truly sees me as a musician.

I don't realize I'm moving until my hand is cupping the side of her face.

"I don't think you realize how much that means to me," I say. "How much *you* mean to me."

"I'm always going to be here for you, Ty," she says softly. "You really are my best friend."

Mel smiles as she leans her head on my shoulder, then pulls it back like she's suddenly remembered something.

"Oh! I forgot—I wanted to show you something."

She flips the pages in her notebook to a song called, *Tonight,* about two people meeting and debating whether or not they should have a one-night stand. We laugh at the subject matter and end up spending the rest of the night editing her lyrics, putting the song to a melody that fits, and talking about more of the music we've made together.

Even though I'm very much engrossed in our work and conversation, I can't stop thinking about the moment we shared earlier.

I don't know what shifted, or why.

I just know that I could sit in this moment with Melody forever.

CHAPTER 7

Melody

I t's Wednesday morning, and I'm sitting in the back of a black truck with my manager, Jaime, on the way to film an episode of *On A High Note*. The podcast is known for interviewing mostly R&B artists and digging into all things music and culture, and sometimes controversy. The hosts, Tammy and KJ, don't shy away from hot topics. Several artists have found themselves trending for the wrong reasons after one of their sound bites went viral on social media.

Jaime prepped me thoroughly. How to talk about my father's death. My previous relationships. Ty and I's sudden rise to fame. And of course, the other famous questions that come up in almost every interview I do.

Are Ty and I dating?

Have we ever dated?

Kissed?

Had sex?

Would we ever date?

It's a side effect of being in a group with a man. People struggle to accept that we have a genuine friendship and do business well together without it turning romantic.

I can't lie, though, after we went out the other night, something switched.

I've been trying to avoid Tyrell, keeping things light and professional. Still, I can't shake thoughts of the way I felt every time I looked into his eyes. Or the way I felt every time his body touched mine as we danced at the lounge.

I've been replaying that night over and over again, and although I can't pinpoint where the attraction started for me, I know that he's crossed my mind way more than I would like to admit. It's nothing to worry about, though. *It doesn't mean anything,* I remind myself. It *can't* mean anything.

"Melody," KJ says, leaning forward. "You're a beautiful woman. Talented. Successful. I'm sure your DMs look crazy."

I immediately laugh, because I know exactly where this comment is heading.

"Well, I have a social media manager," I say. "So, I actually don't see too many of my DMs. Sometimes, she'll show me the craziest ones, and it's usually a marriage proposal or dick pics."

We all crack up at this.

Tammy shakes her head, laughing. "The audacity!"

"So," she continues, "are you dating anyone? The streets wanna know!"

"I definitely wanna know," KJ interjects, which sends me into a laughing fit.

"I'm not dating anyone at the moment," I say, once I catch my breath. "Honestly, I've been so busy, I barely have time to leave my house, let alone meet someone."

Tammy smirks at this, clearly unconvinced.

"And I'm sure you're not in a rush to meet anyone with a group mate as fine as Tyrell sitting right next to you every day."

Here we go.

"Oh my God, guys," I say, covering my face. "I knew this was coming. Tyrell and I are just friends!"

"So, wait," KJ leans back, "Y'all never messed around? Not once?"

I don't hesitate.

"No. Never messed around. Never kissed. Never went out on a date. Never crossed that line."

"And you're telling me you never even thought about it?" Tammy asks with a raised eyebrow.

"No," I say, firm. "I never thought about it. I've dated. He's met the guys I've been with. I've met women he's been with. We've never had any issues because we just don't look at each other like that."

They exchange a look.

"So y'all been friends for a good fifteen years," KJ says, slowly. "Y'all have the same interests. Same career. Same circles. You two have been through real life together. You mean to tell me you wouldn't even consider dating Tyrell?"

I try to be careful with my words.

"Well, I can never say never because I can't predict either one of our futures," I say. "I'll just say maybe, and leave it at that."

KJ's eyes light up.

"Awwww shit, we got a maybe! I *knew* it!"

Tammy smiles. "Melody, he seems like a really good catch. It wouldn't be a bad look for you."

"No, and honestly, Tyrell is a great guy," I admit. "He's incredibly considerate and very sweet. But I'm sure he has plenty of women. I'm not sure I'd want to be a part of that."

I pause, then add, "If I thought he was serious, though, I might at least hear him out."

KJ slaps the table. "We gotta get him up here next so we can see what he has to say about this."

"I'm quite sure he would say the same thing," I say, laughing. "But I appreciate the concern for my love life, though."

"Yo, Tyrell," KJ calls into the mic, "she said maybe. You gotta shoot your shot, bro!"

We all laugh at KJ's animated reaction as Tammy leads us into an R&B Trivia game.

After the podcast wraps, I thank the hosts for their time and step aside with Jaime.

"You know, Mel," she says carefully, "we definitely didn't practice you answering the questions about Tyrell that way."

"I know," I admit. "I just figured it would make things interesting. Just a little something to get people talking and hopefully, tuning into the podcast."

It sounds calculated out loud, even though it wasn't. The truth is, I answered that way because I'm curious too.

It's only a matter of time before Tyrell and I are in the same room again. We share the same job, the same friends, so it's bound to happen. And when it does, what then?

Are we going to keep flirting and then act like it means nothing?

Do we ignore the tension until it goes away?

Or do we risk changing everything?

I don't know which answer to any of these questions scares me more.

CHAPTER 8
Melody

June 2022

"**D**o you really have to leave right now, Mel?"

I smile through my annoyance.

"Yes, Damon. I do." I pull my panties back on while searching for my bra, deliberately avoiding the puppy dog-eyes that he loves to give me when he wants me to stay. "Tyrell and I have a rehearsal. We're playing a wedding next Saturday."

Damon and I have been dating for four months now. What started as a friends-with-benefits situation somehow turned into sleepovers, dinners, and expectations I never asked for. I like Damon, but not enough to take him seriously. He's way too clingy, for one, and worse, he's very dismissive of my music career. Any time I mention something music-related, it's met with pushback or negativity.

"Full-time social worker," he says, stretching lazily across the bed, "part-time wedding singer. It's growing on me, you know."

I would really love to knock the smug look off his face, but

I remind myself that his dick is magical and I'd like to enjoy it for just a little while longer.

Still, sarcasm coats my tone when I respond.

"My work doesn't need to grow on you, Damon. I'm happy with my career choices."

If he actually supported me in this, I might want to keep him around for longer than a late-night fuck.

"I just don't want you to work so hard, baby," he says. "I can take care of you. That way, you're not singing for chump change on the weekends. I don't want my girl living like that."

I stop what I'm doing.

"Okay, first of all, I'm not *your* girl." I pull on my t-shirt and grab my sneakers. "Second, I don't appreciate you down-playing something I love. I love singing. I love performing for people during their special moments. And one day, it will lead to something bigger. Until then, I'm content with what Tyrell and I have built. I don't know why the fuck it's such an issue for you, but I'm sick of hearing you criticize my choices."

At this point, I don't even care how good the dick is. It's not good enough to keep explaining myself to a man who refuses to respect my passion.

Damon jumps out of bed in nothing but his boxer briefs, rushing to me, taking my hand in his.

"Babe. That's not what I meant. I just...I don't want you to put so much into something that's not really going anywhere. The studio time. The rehearsals. I know you, Tyrell, and the band are really into your music, but let's face it. You're thirty now. It's going to be really hard for you to make it in the business at this point."

I release his hand, no longer feeling the need to defend my passion.

"You know what, Damon?" I grab my bag and head to the door. "I think I'm over this. I'm out."

"So, you're just going to leave and run to Tyrell?"

I turn back to him, displeasure in my expression.

"What the fuck is that supposed to mean?"

"Every time we have a disagreement, you go running to that nigga," he snaps. "You call it 'music' or 'work,' or whatever other bullshit excuse you can think of. If you want to be with him, Mel, just say that shit."

"I keep telling you that Tyrell and I are just friends and have been friends for over ten years now. We make music together, and we have a lot of the same friends. He's going to be around whether you like it or not."

Now, Damon's expression matches mine, and the disapproval of my words is evident.

"You fucking him, Mel?"

"No," I say without hesitation. "And even if I was, it wouldn't be any of your business. I'm not your girlfriend. Or did you forget that part?"

Damon takes a deep breath, fingers pressing into his temple.

"You're right," he says. "Because no woman I call my girlfriend would be so wrapped up in another man."

"Whatever, Damon." I'm almost at the door when his next words stop me in my tracks.

"You're in love with him, Mel."

I turn slowly.

"You're so invested in this 'music' thing because it's your connection to Tyrell," he continues. "It's beyond just a friendship, and everyone sees it but the two of you."

"So that's what this is about?" I plant my hands on my hips and step closer. He's towering over me at 6'3", but that doesn't stop me from getting in his face.

"Melody, look me in my face and tell me you don't care about Tyrell."

"Of course, I care about him, Damon! He's one of my closest friends."

He looks away to the side, rolling his eyes at me in the process.

"Look in my eyes, Melody," he says again, "and tell me that you've never thought about being with him. And I'm not talking about as a friend, either."

I could look Damon in his eyes and say that I've never thought about being with Tyrell.

But it wouldn't be true.

I've thought about the possibility of Tyrell and me being together since college. Every late night we spent working. Every song and melody we wrote. Every open mic night we sang duets at. Every inside joke we've shared has all become a culmination of my feelings for a man I swore I would never look at as anything more than a friend. On more than one occasion, I've envisioned myself as Tyrell's girlfriend. I've imagined what it would be like to kiss him. To make love to him. To choose him out loud.

I've put it all in the back of my mind, deciding that a friendship like the one Ty and I share is invaluable. Risking that friendship has always felt too dangerous.

So yeah, Damon is right.

But I won't give him that satisfaction.

"You're wrong, Damon," I say quickly. "Take care of yourself. Don't call me again."

I leave his apartment, ignoring his deep voice calling after me.

I'm not ready to confront the truth of his words.

Not now, and maybe not ever.

The podcast airs the next evening, and my phone immediately starts lighting up with texts from the group chat I share with Tisha, Sydney, and Kim.

KIM

Did y'all watch Mel's episode of On A High Note? Our girl might finally give Ty some play!

SYD

I know you lying! It's about damn time.

TISHA

Mel is just chatting, y'all. She's not paying that man any mind.

Thank you, Tish! I had to say something to make the interview interesting. Nothing to see here...

I toss my phone on the couch beside me and turn my attention back to *Love Jones*, which I'm watching for the 7495'th time. I know every line. Every beat. Every look exchanged between Nina and Darius.

And still.

As the movie plays, my thoughts drift to Tyrell. I hadn't really considered how he'd feel about the interview, about me speaking on his personal life, even in passing. The longer I sit with it, the more my stomach tightens.

As if I summoned him, my phone starts ringing at 10:04 pm.

I don't even have to look at the screen.

I take a deep breath, hoping to exhale the nerves out of my body before they travel through the phone.

Here we go, I think, and swipe right.

"Hey."

"Hey," he says. "I saw the interview you did for *On A High Note* today."

"Oh yeah?" I let out a playful laugh, trying to make it sound harmless. "What'd you think?"

There's a pause on the other end, followed by a matching chuckle.

"You said some really interesting things. I figured I'd call and see how much of that was true."

"Tyrell, you know I'd never use my platform—our platform—to lie about something the public could eat up and feed off of. Every word was true."

"Well, for the record," he says, "I hate that you think I'm some type of player that sleeps with anything walking just because I'm single."

I shift on the couch.

"Oh, so you just skipped over the part where I said you're thoughtful and sweet to me?"

"Did it ever occur to you that maybe you've been getting preferential treatment?"

I freeze.

"Why would you be doing that?"

"Why do you think, Melody?"

My mouth opens, but nothing comes out.

"Ty, I—"

"Why don't I come by tomorrow so we can talk?" he cuts in. "You busy around seven?"

I know I need to be a mature adult about this. An in-person conversation would probably help me sort out whatever this is. Or at least force us to stop dancing around it.

"Seven is fine."

"Good," he says. "I'll see you then. Sweet dreams."

As if I could really sleep with this on my mind.

"Goodnight."

The call ends, and I stare at my phone long after the screen goes dark.

At 7:13 p.m., I press the intercom at Melody's apartment, leaning close enough for my face to fill the screen. A familiar buzz, and the door unlocks.

I step into the elevator and hit seventeen.

My leg won't stop bouncing as the doors slide shut. I force it still, exhaling slowly, like that might help settle the tightness sitting in my chest. I've walked into this building a hundred times without thinking twice, but tonight, I'm suddenly aware of everything—the hum of the elevator, the mirrored walls, the way my palms feel slightly damp.

Tonight is the night I finally have an honest conversation with the woman I've been best friends with, built with, and experienced every high and low of my adult life alongside. Tonight is the night I say what I've been sitting with for days. Tonight is the night I tell Melody how I feel — and ask her on a real date.

I don't knock right away when I reach her door. I stand there for a second longer than usual, then tap out my usual rhythm and wait.

"It's open!" she calls from inside.

When I walk in, I find her in the kitchen, standing over the stove. She looks effortlessly beautiful in a white tank top and linen pants, her hair is straight with loose curls at the ends, and her pink-rimmed cat-eye glasses framing her face. She is strikingly gorgeous in her leisure attire, and I have to catch myself from staring too hard.

I slip my shoes off and follow the scent of whatever she's cooking.

"Hi, Sweetie," she says, leaning in to hug me with one arm, the other hand still holding her wooden spoon.

"Hey, Kitty. What you making?"

I hug her back, my hand settling at the small of her waist for slightly longer than necessary. I catch myself and step aside, pretending I'm just trying to stay out of her way. She doesn't need to know I'm really trying to avoid touching her at all.

Ever since that night out and the podcast interview, I've been looking at Melody through brand-new lenses. I've admired her for years—her talent, the way she shows up for those she loves, and her kindness towards those she doesn't—but now, it feels harder to keep that admiration from showing on my face.

I'm thirty-four years old, standing in my best friend's kitchen with a crush I don't know what to do with. If this ain't some bullshit, I don't know what is.

"Ribeye, a little pasta in a lobster butter sauce, and spinach."

I glance at the stove, my mouth watering. Mel has always been a phenomenal cook. Back in the day when I was dead broke after graduation, trying to land my first job, she made me more meals than I can count.

"You made all this for me?"

"I made all this for *me,*" she says. "You just happen to be here."

Always playing hard to get.

"I'm too hungry to argue with that."

"What else is new?" she teases, smiling at me as she stirs the spinach.

"Anyway," I grab two wine glasses from her wooden cabinet.

"Red or white?"

"Red, please."

I grab the unfinished bottle of Caymus from the wine fridge and pour us both a glass, setting them on the dining table. It's neatly set with china, napkins, and silverware, and the apartment is more spotless than usual.

She prepared for this.

I glance around, then back at her.

"Melody?"

"Hmm?"

"You're nervous, aren't you?"

She presses her lips to the side, a questioning look on her face.

"What would I be nervous about?"

I should've known that was coming. Since I've met Melody, she's always worn her armor well. She makes it a point to never show that she's rattled or bothered by things. Very rarely do you get her to express how she truly feels about something. Usually, that doesn't bother me.

Right now, it does.

I let it go.

"Nothing at all."

She studies me for a split second.

"I think you're the one that's nervous, Tyrell."

"The only thing I'm nervous about is you overcooking my steak. Medium, please."

"You know I've never overcooked anything I've made for you."

She finishes plating the pasta, sprinkling fresh parsley over the top. When she speaks again, her voice is lower—deliberate—and it does exactly what it feels meant to do.

"Everything I serve you is always just right."

She walks past me with our plates, glancing back with a smirk.

I take it as a challenge.

Challenge accepted.

CHAPTER 11

Melody

I'm sitting across from Tyrell at my dining room table, sharing a meal with him, drinking wine, chatting as we always do. To anyone who knows us, this would look completely normal. Familiar, even. Sharing a meal is nothing new for us. Talking about anything and everything is nothing new for us. Laughing at each other's jokes, no matter how corny or inappropriate they are, is definitely nothing new for us.

What *is* new for me, however, is the undeniable pull I feel towards him.

Ever since we went out a few weeks ago—since we spent time just being our old selves—I've been seeing Tyrell differently. Don't get me wrong now, I fully acknowledge that Tyrell has been fine since the day that I met him. 6'2", perfect smile, the cutest single dimple that shows up when he laughs for real. Smooth skin, locs that have grown considerably longer since college, and a body that would make even professional athletes a little jealous.

None of this is new information.

What's new is that I can't ignore it anymore.

That night at the lounge plays in my head more often than I care to admit. The dancing. The staring. The way the rest of the room seemed to fall away until it felt like it was just us two standing there, locked into something unspoken, neither one of us willing to look away first. I really thought he was going to kiss me right there on the dance floor. I would've let him.

When Tammy asked me on the podcast if I'd ever consider dating Tyrell, for once, I didn't derail the question. I answered with an honest 'maybe' because, for the first time, I didn't rule out the possibility.

Now, I'm sitting here, talking about anything I can think of to avoid talking about the one thing we're clearly both thinking about. The elephant has been pacing the room since he walked in, and I refuse to acknowledge him first.

Or at all.

"Mel," Tyrell says, breaking into my thoughts, "you know I came here to talk to you about something."

Damn. Elephant confronted.

"I'm listening."

Tyrell shifts a little in his seat, wiping his hands with his napkin like he needs a second to ground himself. He takes a quick swig of his wine before continuing.

"So, you know when we went out a couple weeks ago...we had a great time. But, it felt different than it usually does."

I keep my face neutral, not letting on that I share mutual feelings about that night.

"How so?"

"You know how, Mel. The dancing. The staring. The whole vibe. It felt like something was happening between us."

Avoid. Avoid. Avoid.

"We both were a little tipsy," I say lightly. "I get a little touchy when I drink."

The look he gives me lets me know he sees right through

my bullshit excuse, and I almost feel bad for trying to deny all of this.

"Neither of us was drunk, and you know that," he says. "I know you felt something, and you know you felt something. You can downplay it if you want, but it was there."

I let out a sigh. He deserves my honesty—even if it scares me.

"You're right," I admit. "I did feel something. That's why I answered the way I did on the podcast."

He reaches across the table and takes my hand in his. A tingle runs through me when he touches me, but I don't take my hand away. I leave it planted in his, a quiet warmth spreading through me that I don't fight.

"Let me take you out on a proper date, Mel," he says. "Just to see if what we're feeling is actually something. No pressure. If it's nothing, we go back to being friends. No expectations."

The sigh I release this time is heavier than the last one, and I decide to make my reservations known.

"I hear what you're saying, Ty. I do. But this is a tricky situation. We've built something solid over the years. Crossing that line changes things. And change isn't always good."

He tilts his head to the side, studying me for a moment.

"What are you afraid of?"

"Everything."

"Let me take you to dinner on Saturday. Show you there's nothing to be afraid of."

"Why now?" I ask. "Why are you doing this, Tyrell?"

"Because," he pauses, then says it plainly.

"I can't stop thinking about you. And I know your ass has been thinking about me too, so don't even sit here and try to lie."

I snicker at the audacity of him to call me out like that.

"I've thought about you some, yeah."

"Enough to matter."

"That doesn't mean we need to go out on a date, though."

"Why are you so scared of one date with me? Afraid you might really fall for me?"

At this, I cackle.

"You clearly don't know me as well as you think."

"I'm not playing games with you," he says. "I like you more than a friend. I want to see if there's something more here."

"I'm not an experiment that you can just decide you want to test out because you feel like you can. I'm a real person, you know."

I roll my eyes at Ty for dramatic effect.

"And I've known that about you for a long time. All of the qualities that I want in a woman, I see in you."

"Ty...I'm flattered by that. You're an amazing man. Kind, thoughtful, considerate, funny, fun to be around. Incredibly talented."

"You forgot to say sexy."

"Yes, you are very handsome," I shake my head, smiling. "Just because there's an attraction doesn't mean we need to explore it," I say quietly. "We've been good friends for a long time, Ty. Really good. That kind of bond doesn't come around often, and once it changes...You can't undo it. Why risk breaking something that's been working?"

He doesn't answer right away. When he does, his voice is steady, but there's something under it. Something careful.

"Because it's more than an attraction," he says. "I don't just see you as a beautiful woman. I see *you*. The way you've loved and cared for me over the years. The way you show up. The passion you pour into your craft, even when no one's watching. The way we can talk about anything and be ourselves around one another. All of it is real, and it all matters."

He exhales, rubbing a hand over his jaw like he's trying not to say too much. "Don't make me beg, girl."

He smiles then, that earnest, disarming smile that's always been my undoing. I take in his features. Chiseled jawline, high cheekbones, beautiful eyes. *Damn.*

"You make it very hard to say no to you," I admit.

"Just one date," he says. "It could suck, you know."

I scoff. "You know damn well it won't, Tyrell."

"We'll cross that bridge when we get there," he says.

He sets his napkin on the table and stands, stepping closer until I have to tilt my head up to look at him.

"Thank you for dinner," he says. "I'm sorry I can't stay longer. Promised G I'd hit some networking event with him downtown."

"I forgive you for not doing the dishes this time."

He leans down to kiss my cheek—familiar, gentle, and somehow heavier than it's ever been.

"I'll make it up to you," he murmurs. "See you tomorrow, Kitty."

It's the night of my first date with Melody, which is still strange to even think about. I've spent the better part of my adulthood orbiting this woman—working with her, laughing with her, trusting her with the parts of myself I don't hand over easily. And yet, the amount of sheer nervousness I feel at this moment is highly uncharacteristic.

I try to pinpoint why. Part of it is obvious: what if we just don't click on a romantic level like I thought we would? Would I be able to just ignore the feelings that I have for Melody and go back to being platonic friends? That would certainly make doing business together awkward. It wouldn't be impossible, but it wouldn't be simple either.

Still, there's another possibility sitting right beside that fear. There's an even bigger chance that this woman might in fact be my soulmate. That the thing I've been searching for, without realizing it, has been standing in front of me this whole time.

That thought is both scary and satisfying.

All of these thoughts seem to gather in my head at once

while I'm driving to Melody's apartment. We only live twenty-five minutes away from one another, but the drive feels like five. When I knock on her door, flowers in hand, I'm ready for whatever this night brings.

She opens the door, and my jaw nearly drops.

Mel looks absolutely stunning.

She's dressed in a long black silk gown that hugs her just right, paired with black heels, adding to her height. Her hair is parted to the side, smooth and glossy, with soft waves framing her face. Minimal jewelry. Effortless. Chic.

"Hi, Sweetie," she says.

Her voice is lower than usual, a raspiness that I wasn't prepared for. I lean in to hug her, pressing a gentle kiss on her forehead, grounding myself in the familiarity of her before my thoughts run wild.

"You look gorgeous, Kitty," I tell her honestly. "Got your hair done for me?"

She looks up at me and swats my shoulder. "No, silly. I did it myself. But thank you."

"Fasho. You look good," I say. "And I like the shoes with the dress."

"Yeah?" She shrugs. "I wanted to wear gold sandals, but I couldn't find the pair I was thinking of. I don't love my outfit, but I'll get over it."

"You look beautiful, regardless," I say, meaning every word. "And these are for you."

I hand her the flowers—a last-minute order of a carefully arranged mix of pink lilies, red roses, and red and pink hydrangeas that I had to negotiate with my florist for.

Melody beams at the sight of the flowers.

"These are so beautiful!" she says. "Thank you, I love them."

She walks to the kitchen, and I study her body as she

moves. The switch of her hips as she walks in her heels. The back muscles peeking out of her backless dress, revealing two dimples in her lower back. The Sankofa tattoo at the small of her back, standing out against her rich, deep chocolate skin.

I turn my head so she doesn't notice the severity of my physical attraction to her.

"Don't read the card yet," I say, needing a distraction.

She laughs. "Okay. I'm not even going to ask."

"Good. Are you ready?"

"Ready."

The drive is quiet. Too quiet.

Melody has never been one to shy away from conversation, but tonight she's watching the city pass by, her thoughts clearly elsewhere. Silence passes between us for longer than I can stand, and I finally speak up.

"You okay?"

She turns to me. "I'm good. Why?"

"You're too quiet."

"I'm just taking in the views."

I twist my mouth up at her and roll my eyes. "Seriously, Mel?"

Her small laugh fills the space, and her eyes immediately relax. "Okay, fine. I'm just a little nervous. I don't know why, but I am."

"We've gone out to dinner a million times. This is really no different. What are you nervous about?"

I rest my hand on her thigh, giving it a slight squeeze that's meant to reassure her. Instead, I feel the firmness of her toned muscle beneath the silk dress, and I wonder what the real thing might feel like. I immediately have to check myself.

I guess I shouldn't blame Mel for being nervous, because this *is* different.

Her low voice breaks me out of my trance. "I don't know. What if it's awkward? What if we run out of things to say? And then there's the kiss at the end of the night, and that's always an awkward situation, but it's going to be even more awkward for us because we're friends and I ju—"

"Slow down," I cut in, amused. "As much as you love to run your mouth, we would never not have anything to talk about. And you're nervous about a kiss that doesn't have to happen tonight at all."

She looks unconvinced.

"Unless," I add, "if you're that nervous about it, let's get it out of the way now."

She blinks, giving me a confused look. "Wait, what?"

"Kiss me right now. Then we don't have to think about it again. I can't have you being weird all night."

"Tyrell, you're crazy," she says, humor filling her voice.

I pull the car over without another word, put the car in park, and quickly unbuckle my seatbelt.

"Oh," she says. "You're serious about this."

"I am."

"If it's a bad kiss, at least I get to tease you about it all through dinner. Like, relentlessly. And if it's a good kiss, then we just...don't even have to talk about it, and we can enjoy the rest of the night. Cool?"

She looks at me, waiting.

"Only you would come up with something like that," she shakes her head, smiling. "But fine."

The setting sun pours through the car's panoramic sunroof, casting her in warm light. She looks unreal. Her skin emits a glow that makes her look radiant, and the curiosity in her eyes makes it hard to look anywhere else. I lift her chin gently and place a soft kiss on her even softer lips. Slow, like I'm giving us both room to pull back.

Neither of us does.

I kiss her again, deeper this time, parting my mouth to let our tongues meet, my hand sliding to the back of her head as our mouths move together, familiar and new all at once. The taste of her tongue and the warmth of her mouth send a fire through me. When I slowly pull away, I press one last kiss to her lips.

"See?" I smile, voice low and deep. "Easy."

Melody looks at me, and whatever she's feeling is written all over her face. Longing and maybe...lust? Her lips stay slightly parted, like she's waiting to see what I'll do next.

"Yeah," she says quietly. "Easy."

Nothing about her feels easy. The air between us thickens, heavy and slow, and for a second, I swear I can feel her breathing match mine. I stay close, closer than I should, close enough to remember exactly how her mouth felt on mine and how much I want it again.

The seductiveness in her eyes almost makes me want to turn the car around and head back to her place. Neither one of us is ready for that...yet.

I drag my thumb along her thigh, giving it another squeeze before I take my hand back and reach for my seatbelt. Not because I want to—but because if I don't, I won't stop.

"Can you be normal now?" I say, attempting to cool the mood.

"Shut up," she laughs, hitting me on the leg. "You're a good kisser, by the way."

"I don't like how surprised you sound by that," I say, grinning.

"I'm more relieved than I am surprised," she counters. "Your confidence could've definitely backfired."

"It rarely does," I turn to glance at Melody as we sit at a red light. "I have a lot to be confident about."

She shakes her head, smiling as she says, "I'd have to see it to believe it."

It's going to be a great night.

If it wasn't for the cowl neck detail on my dress, Ty would've seen *exactly* how I felt about that kiss.

I wasn't expecting him to pull the car over and kiss me right then and there, but...*shit*. The way his lips fit so perfectly against mine. The way he gave me just the right amount of tongue. The way he took his time and wasn't overly aggressive. Gentle, but firm. It was the perfect kiss, and it is nearly impossible for me not to think about it, or kissing him again, or him kissing me all over...

"This is the restaurant on the right, Mel. You ready?"

Ty's voice pulls me from my inappropriate thoughts. I nod, sifting through my purse for my lip gloss and liner, suddenly hyper-aware of my mouth. I feel his eyes on me.

"Do you have to watch me while I do this?"

"I'm just taking in the views."

I roll my eyes, and we both laugh at him mocking me with my same comment from earlier. He gives his keys to the valet, then circles the car to open my door, extending his hand to help me out of his Porsche. His hand rests on the small of my back as he guides me inside.

These gestures aren't new—Ty has always been a gentleman—but I appreciate them a little more now.

There are things about me that Ty already knows.

When we're out at restaurants, he knows that if he lets me order for myself, I'll change my mind at least twice because I'm indecisive. He knows that any time I drink beer, it always has to be out of a glass. He knows which sparkling water I prefer without asking. He knows if there are crab cakes on the menu, I'm ordering them. He knows that he has to read me the menu because I forgot to bring my glasses. He knows if there's anything banana-flavored on the dessert menu, I want it.

These aren't first-date discoveries. They're the result of years.

He knows things about me that have taken time to learn, and I recognize the luxury of a familiarity that allows us to be casual on the first date. There's no performance here. No learning curve. We can just be ourselves, which is as refreshing to me as a cool beverage on a sweltering day.

The hostess leads us to a booth tucked in the back, and we take seats across from one another. Although I feel more relaxed after our kiss, I'm suddenly self-conscious again, smoothing my hair and checking if my makeup is okay, while pretending to read from the cocktail menu I can't actually see.

"Don't tell me you're still nervous."

"I'm not! I'm just fixing my hair."

"Your hair is fine," he says easily. "And you're holding that menu like you can actually see. It's a dead giveaway."

"If you weren't staring at me so hard, you wouldn't even notice."

"I notice everything about you without me even trying to, Melody. When you've had fifteen years to study someone, you tend to pick up on things."

His words land deep.

As much as I want to swoon over him, I hold it together. Barely.

"You're really running your best game tonight," I say lightly. "I'm kind of impressed."

"I have never run game on a woman," he replies. "This is natural charm."

I roll my eyes, smiling despite myself.

"Speaking of charm...what's up with you and Natalie?"

"You don't waste any time, huh?" he exhales. "We haven't even ordered drinks yet."

"I'm not going to beat around the bush with you, Tyrell. I know you."

"That's fair." He pauses. "Honestly, I'm not into her. Something's missing. She's really nice, beautiful, smart...but the chemistry isn't there. I feel like I can't be myself with her."

"And you've communicated this to her?"

"Not yet," he admits. "But I intend to. To be honest, I don't really know how to say it. How do you tell someone that really likes you and that you've spent time with, that you're no longer interested in them? I don't want to hurt her feelings."

I sigh. "You don't think it's more hurtful to keep stringing her along?"

"I know." He looks at me intently. "I have other priorities at the moment."

"Which are?"

He doesn't hesitate.

"I'm sitting across from my biggest one."

The look he gives me isn't playful. Our eyes meet for what feels like an eternity, and in that moment, both of our intentions feel clear.

Our waiter appears before I can respond. "Have you had a chance to look at the drink menu?" he asks.

Without discussion, Ty orders our dinner and drinks,

choosing everything from the menu that he knows I'd be a fan of, all of which sounds incredibly appetizing.

It's at this point that I recognize two truths: this man knows me more than I thought, and I'm more caught up in him than I realized.

Dinner goes smoothly. We talk about family. We talk about politics. We talk about music. We talk about movies. We talk like friends would talk, cracking jokes, laughing, smiling, shameless flirting, the occasional brush of his fingers against mine that feels entirely too intimate for something so small.

It's the perfect date, and I can't help but feel giddy as we step outside, my hand in his, my body warm despite the cool LA air. His hands settle at my hips while we wait for the valet, grounding and possessive in a way that makes my pulse stutter.

I'm full. Relaxed. A little drunk on fruity cocktails and attention.

And painfully aware that if I don't pull myself out of this blissful state, I'm going to wake up tomorrow morning with Tyrell naked in my bed.

And I don't know if I'd regret it at all.

I park in the guest spot in Mel's garage and turn the engine off, sitting in the quiet for half a beat longer than necessary.

"Let me just walk you upstairs and make sure you get in safely," I offer, my tone steady. The truth is that I'm not ready for this night to end.

Between the conversations on all of the things that we want out of our own lives, politics, music, and our jokes and banter, dinner was just...*easy*. There was no show for me to put on, no trying to gauge whether or not I was saying or doing the right things, and no wondering how she could be feeling about me. We talked the way we always have—only now, there was an undercurrent to it. Something charged. Something that lingered every time her hand brushed mine, or her eyes held mine a second too long.

I don't want to break that thread yet.

"I'm fine, Sweetie," she says easily. Then, her eyes light up. "Oh! But come up anyway. You can help me eat some of these desserts I got earlier."

Sweetie.

She calls everyone that. Family. Friends. The kids she mentors.

But something about the way she says it right now makes me feel like it means more. Like it's meant just for me.

Get a fucking grip, Ty.

The elevator ride is quiet, but comfortable. I glance at her, taking in the soft sway of her body, the faint flush still warming her skin.

"You look like you might've had a little too much to drink."

Clearly, teasing her is my way of both flirting with her and calming my nerves.

"I had just as much as you did," she shoots back, stepping off ahead of me. "And actually, I wouldn't mind another one."

"Damn," I say, smirking. "Was the date that bad that you need to drink to forget about it?"

I am mostly teasing, but slightly curious to know how she feels about how things went. Are going. Is the date still going on?

I really need to get out of my head. Another drink might not be a bad idea.

She turns to look at me, expression flat, but eyes sharp. "If you couldn't tell that I had a good time, then you are clearly oblivious."

She says it so matter-of-factly. I have to stop myself from closing the distance to kiss her.

"Whatever, Kitty," I mutter, using her old nickname from college days to get under her skin a little.

She rolls her eyes, but the corner of her mouth lifts as she unlocks her door.

"I'm gonna change my clothes," she says casually. "I'll be right back."

"You need help?" I ask with a smirk. The pep talk I just gave myself already went out the door.

Her eyebrow lifts as she looks back at me. A challenge. A warning. A promise.

"All good," she says, smirking as she disappears down the hallway.

I exhale slowly and run a hand over my face.

We are playing a very dangerous game.

I move toward the kitchen—anticipating the moment she's back out here with me—my attention tuned entirely to the sounds of her moving in the other room. Drawers opening. Fabric shifting. The quiet hum of her apartment wrapping around me.

Every instinct in me says *slow down*.

Every other one says *don't waste this moment*.

And I have a feeling Melody knows that too.

I wanted to tell him that I did need help—in more ways than one—but saying nothing felt like the safest thing to do.

As I walked toward my bedroom, I could feel his eyes watching my every move. I made sure to slow my steps to give him the show I knew he was desperately craving.

What the fuck are you doing, Melody?

I close my bedroom door behind me and lean against it for a second, breathing out slowly. My pulse is louder than it should be. I slip out of my dress and hang it carefully in my closet, like taking my time might help me get my thoughts back under control before I start some shit between us that we can't come back from.

We had an amazing date. From the kiss in the car—which I still felt on my lips—to the incredible food, to the way the conversation flowed so easily, it made hours disappear. It was fulfilling in a way that made me feel like I didn't want it to end. I'm on a high—and not because of the drinks—but because it made me want *more*. More time. More closeness. More of him.

I'd spent years telling myself that whatever spark Tyrell and

I had was harmless. Manageable. Something I could keep tucked away without consequence. But now that we'd acknowledged it—even just a little—I wasn't so sure I could put it back where it belonged.

The chemistry that I always suspected was there wasn't imaginary. It was real. And sitting just outside my bedroom door.

I know we need to do the responsible thing. Take our time, sort out our feelings, and figure out what, if anything, is happening between us. But responsibility feels abstract right now, and I can't help but be curious about the sexual tension that's building between us.

The sound of thunder shakes me out of my thoughts, loud enough to make me jump. I turn toward my windows to see heavy rain rapidly coming down, sheets of it blurring the city lights below. My first thought surprised me.

I have an excuse to ask him to stay.

It would be rude to have him drive twenty-five minutes back to his apartment in the midst of a torrential downpour, right? That wasn't me. I'd never do that to someone I cared about.

And I *did* care about him.

Decision made, I change into a soft t-shirt and lounge pants, something comfortable but not careless. As I pulled them on, I remembered the pair of Ty's sweatpants I still had tucked away from years ago, back when we threw him a surprise birthday party. I told myself it was practical to keep them.

I told myself a lot of things.

If he is going to stay, I should at least make sure he's comfortable. That was just common courtesy. The friendly thing to do. And Ty and I are...friends.

Right? Right.

I pick up the sweatpants and exhale slowly, knowing I'm not backing away from this moment—I'm stepping into it.

Mel steps out of her bedroom in lounge pants and a white t-shirt that clings to her body in a way that feels unfair. My eyes drift, landing on her breasts —and that's when I notice the piercings.

Oh. She's teasing me, and she knows it.

Despite myself, I nod toward them. "When did you get those?"

Her cheeks flush a little, and I realize she might be embarrassed. *Oh, shit*—I might've misread this entirely. Maybe she wasn't trying to tease me at all. Maybe she just threw on the first shirt she saw, and now I'm here sexualizing her and making things awkward. We're supposed to be friends, and I'm blatantly just lusting over her.

I immediately regret my ill-mannered question, and am about to open my mouth to apologize when she laughs.

"Oh!" she says, shaking her head. "Tisha and I got these done two years ago. We were out drinking, and she had the bright idea that we should get piercings. I tried to get out of it by getting a third hole in my ears, but somehow she convinced me that putting holes in my titties was a better idea."

At this, we both laugh, and I'm grateful for Mel's ability to lighten the mood.

"Tisha's freaky ass would suggest some shit like that," I start. "I'm sorry for being so frank, too. I was caught off guard. I hope I didn't make you uncomfortable."

She looks at me in a way that tells me she appreciates my sincerity, and I again appreciate my friend. She has always been patient with me, even when I fuck up.

"Ty," she says quietly, "you could never make me uncomfortable."

The air shifts after that. Not heavy, just charged.

We stare at each other for too long after she says this. We're standing close now, closer than we need to be, and the silence between us says more than any words can fill. It's at this moment that I can tell she wants this as much as I do.

She finally breaks the silence, lifting the sweatpants she's holding in her hand—*my* sweatpants. I recognize them immediately.

"I found these in my closet from your birthday party," she says. "I thought you might want them in case you wanted to get more comfortable...if you wanted to stay the night. Because of the rain, you know."

I almost laugh at her flimsy excuse.

I step closer to her, close enough to kiss her. My voice drops without effort.

"Melody...do you want me to stay the night?"

She pauses, carefully considering her answer. Then she rises onto her toes, leaning in just enough to whisper seductively in my ear,

"What kind of dessert did you think I was inviting you up for?"

My eyes widen, and it takes everything in me not to lay her across this counter.

I straighten slowly, fighting the instinct to pull her into me. "I was hoping for something with cream in the middle." I play her game as well as I can.

She backs up and heads to her fridge. "It's strawberry cheesecake, nasty ass."

She pulls out a green Emerald's Bakery box to reveal two slices of strawberry cheesecake, both topped with whipped cream. She's laughing at me, and I can't help but laugh, too.

"That's the cream I was talking about," I say smoothly. "The whipped cream."

"Nice try," she says, handing me a fork. "That was smooth though."

"Ha," I attempt to play it off. "I forgot who I was playing with."

As she takes the first bite, she looks me over—really looks—and smirks.

"I don't think you have any idea who you're playing with, Tyrell."

Yeah.

She won this round.

CHAPTER 17

Melody

We make our way to the living room with our plates of cake, settling onto opposite ends of the couch—but "opposite" is generous. There's barely any space between us. The lights are dimmed low, soft music playing in the background, and suddenly, my apartment feels smaller. Warmer. Charged.

For someone who's been telling herself all night that she *doesn't* want to send the wrong message, the setting in here is doing an excellent job of contradicting me.

I tell myself to just relax. To breathe.

Our playful banter has turned into something else entirely—full out flirting full of innuendos and glances, words that feel like they're carrying more meaning than they should. It's getting to be too much, even for me. One of us needs to be mature about this. One of us needs to remember the boundary between us.

Tyrell and I are just friends.

I repeat it like a mantra, hoping it might eventually stick. I mean...technically, it's true. We're just friends who share a deep attraction, common interests and values, the same sense of humor, the same rhythm. Friends who can spend hours talking without getting bored. We are no different than any other pair of friends just hanging out on a Saturday night.

Nothing to worry about.

"What are you thinking about? You're quiet over there," he says, his voice gentle, but inquisitive.

It would be easy to flirt my way out of answering. Easy to deflect. But something about the way he's looking at me makes me choose restraint instead.

"Nothing," I say lightly. "Would you like a drink?"

"Please. I'll have whatever you're having."

Now, he's being too formal. I need to stop overthinking this.

"You know, you're no longer a visitor," I say. "You should be the one making the drinks."

He laughs, already standing. "Yo, how you gonna offer me a drink and then scold me for not making it myself?"

In the kitchen, I hand him two limes and pull the bourbon from the cabinet. The simple act of moving around each other —passing close, brushing arms—feels deliberate, even though neither of us says a word about it. I mix something sweet and strong, exactly what I need right now.

When I slide his glass toward him, I hold the spoon up to his lips. "Taste."

He hums after a sip. "This is good. Strong, too."

"Awww. Do I need to add some juice to yours?"

"Don't insult me," he says, rolling his eyes at me.

"Cheers," I say, and we clink our glasses.

"Ooo," I wince slightly after my first sip. "Ok, yeah. This *is* strong."

"Told you," he says. "I think you're just trying to get me drunk so you can keep talking shit and getting away with it."

He's not wrong.

"You want the truth?" I ask. I'm done pretending.

He nods.

"I just wanted an excuse to keep you here longer. I didn't want the night to end."

It's vulnerable and defies all of the logic needed at the moment, but it's my truth.

"I didn't want it to end either, Kitty."

He moves closer, close enough that our shoulders brush. The contact is barely there, but it sends heat straight through me.

"I had a really good time tonight."

"Yeah," I reply quietly. "I did too."

I take a long sip of my drink, mostly to keep myself from saying too much. From saying everything...

"Dance with me."

Rufus & Chaka Khan's *Everlasting Love* fills the room right on queue. He holds out his hand. I shake my head, hesitating just for a second, then put my hand in his.

He leads me to the center of the living room, one hand on the small of my back, the other around my waist. My body responds instantly, heat blooming everywhere he touches, and I do my best to show restraint.

As we sway slowly, barely moving, I slide my arms around his neck, aware of how easily I fit there. It feels odd to be near him in this way. Sure, we've danced together before—crowded rooms, loud music, bodies everywhere—but this is different. There's no audience. No distractions.

Just Us.

This feels much more...intimate.

This feels right.

CHAPTER 18

Tyrell

We move together in an unhurried rhythm, staring into each other's eyes. Neither of us speaks. We don't need to. The music fills the space just enough to give us something to move to, but all of my attention is on her.

"You are so beautiful," I say quietly.

It isn't clever or smooth, but it's the truth. Even in the low lights, Melody seems to glow, her skin warm and luminous beneath my hands. I don't allow myself to overthink the words or worry about how they'll land. I simply accept that Mel will grasp how much her beauty—her entire being—is affecting me at this moment. I just let them exist between us, because she deserves to hear them.

"Thank you," she replies with a soft smile.

My chest tightens. Now is my chance.

"Would I be overstepping if I kissed you?"

I am half expecting hesitation, half expecting a joke. Anything but what she gives me.

"I've been waiting all night for you to kiss me again."

That does it. I'm ignited in more ways than one, and the restraint I've been holding onto snaps clean in half.

I lift her chin gently and kiss her, savoring the moment. Her lips are just as soft as I remember, sending a dash of electricity through me. I pull away instinctively, barely an inch, but she's already reaching for me, her hands sliding up my face as she pulls me right back in.

This kiss is different. Hungrier. Our mouths move together with intention now, tongues learning each other in a way that feels inevitable. The fullness of Mel's body in my hands activates my own desires. She fits against mine so naturally that it almost steals my breath. I kiss along her jaw, down her neck, and wherever else she'll allow, breathing her in.

I want more. I want all of her. I need her...now. I am craving her, but I force myself to stop.

"Mel," I say, my voice rougher than I intend. "Wait."

She looks at me, eyes dark, lips swollen, breath uneven.

"Are you sure you want to do this?"

"I'm sure," she answers without hesitation.

I don't ask twice.

She takes my hand and leads me toward her bedroom, her fingers laced with mine like she's done it a hundred times before. We don't stop kissing as we go. I fumble with my jacket, with my shirt, too eager, until I feel her hand on my chest.

"Slow down," she teases, soft but certain. "We have all night."

The sound of it, the promise in her tone, nearly makes me explode.

She's right.

And she's worth the wait.

CHAPTER 19

Melody

I slow Tyrell down because even though I want him—badly—I'm still nervous. I break our kiss and turn away just long enough to open my drawer, my hands slightly unsteady as I search. When I find it, I pull out a gold Magnum and walk back to him.

"Think you can fit this?"

His mouth curves into a cocky grin. Without a word, he steps back and slides his pants down slowly, like he's giving me a show. He follows with his boxer briefs and then just stands there, naked, confident, not saying a word.

"*Damn.*"

I take him in fully. His brown skin looks like it was hand-dipped in the smoothest caramel. Defined abs, broad shoulders, and toned legs. And the proof of his confidence—eight inches of girthy dick standing at attention in front of me. If he was trying to make a point, it landed. Loud and clear.

"That's what I thought," he says as he steps closer, fingers tugging the waistband of my pants. Gently, he lifts my shirt over my head, his eyes darkening as my bare breasts are revealed, nipples on full display, piercings catching the light.

The look on his face—like it's his first meal on Thanksgiving Day and I'm the yams and the mac—makes my breath hitch.

He lays me back onto the bed, taking his time as he removes my pants. His fingers trail slowly from my lips, down the center of my chest, over my stomach, until they rest against the soft lace of my pink thong.

"You're beautiful, Mel," he says softly, his gaze sweeping over me, admiration in his eyes.

Before I can respond, he leans down to kiss me—deep and measured—our tongues dancing as we run our hands all over each other's bodies. He breaks the kiss and moves lower, his mouth closing around my breast, his tongue circling my left nipple until a moan slips from my lips. He does the same to the right, then continues downward, planting soft kisses on my body, from my breasts, to my navel, to my panty line, deliberate and teasing.

It's too much, and not enough. I reach for him, my fingers threading into his locs, guiding him lower.

"Don't fucking rush me, Melody," he says, his voice husky and deep, instantly making my juices flow.

He's staring into my soul as he unhurriedly slides my panties down my legs and discards them on the floor. He slips two of his fingers down my center, using the evidence of my arousal to draw slow circles over my clit.

"Ty, please," I beg.

I barely have time to inhale before he pushes those same two fingers into my mouth, the want clear in his eyes. "Find something to do with that mouth of yours," he growls, "and I'll do the same."

He dips his head between my thighs and explores my pussy with his lips and tongue. Every sensation stacks on top of the last, and I feel my orgasm building almost immediately. His tongue hits spots I didn't even know existed, moving like he knows exactly what he's doing—exactly how to undo me. I grip the sheets, and it doesn't take long before I'm on the edge of losing control.

"Fuck, Ty!" I let out, as my legs shake, and my point of ecstasy is reached.

When he finally raises his head, our eyes lock. The way he's looking at me—dark, focused, promising—tells me everything.

Whatever I just started, there's no turning back now.

He's about to fuck me up, and I'm too far gone to do anything about it.

I lick my lips, savoring the last of Mel's juices on my tongue, and it nearly drives me insane. She tastes just as sweet as I always imagined—it's intoxicating. And the way she soaked my mouth when she came has me more than eager to get inside of her, my restraint hanging on by a thread.

I kiss her deeply as I roll the condom on, spreading her legs in the process. She's so wet that despite my size, I slide in easily, and it takes everything in me not to cum inside of her. Her warmth and tightness wraps around me like her body knows mine already.

I slowly begin to stroke her, going a little deeper each time, forcing myself to pace it. Her arms hook around my back, nails scratching my skin, urging me on. When I look down, her eyes meet mine, and she grabs my face to kiss me, soft in a way that wrecks me more than anything else.

"You could've told me your shit was this good, baby," I growl into her ear, picking up my pace.

"Damn...Ty," she moans. "You're gonna make me cum again."

Her legs begin to tremble, and I slow my pace down on purpose, holding her right there.

"I didn't tell you it was time to cum yet, Melody."

I bite her nipple, licking it slowly, watching her body react, watching her try not to lose it.

"Fuuuuuuck baby," she moans. "You feel soooo good."

Her breathing turns ragged, desperate. I push deeper, my rhythm stronger now, and just as I feel her climax nearing—

I pull out.

"W-what the fuck, Tyrell?" Mel is staring at me in half confusion, half bliss, her body squirming beneath mine.

I lean down, lips pressed against her ear, my words low and firm. "You cum when I tell you to."

I slide back into her slowly, setting a pace that makes her beg. It doesn't take long before she's shaking again.

"Oh, shit! Right there," she whines. "Right there."

"Cum for me, baby," I coach, gripping her thigh with one hand, my other hand steady at her throat—just enough to remind her who she belongs to in this moment.

"Fuuuuuuck, Ty!"

Mel erupts beneath me, her body clenching around me, and the sound she makes pushes me right to the edge. I quickly flip her over, directing her where I want her to be, and enter her from behind. The way she arches into me, the way her moans climb with every stroke, sends me spiraling.

"Fuck, Mel!" I groan. "You feel so good, baby."

I can't hold back anymore. I grip her waist, my pace losing all restraint now, and when I finally cum, the sound I make is raw, unfiltered, loud enough that I'm sure the neighbors hear us, but I don't care.

We collapse together on the bed, breathing hard, like we just completed a marathon.

When our eyes meet, I laugh softly, still trying to catch my breath. She smiles right back, slow and satisfied.

"Damn, Mel."

"I would've given you some years ago if I knew you could put it down like that," she says, moving a few locs away from my face.

"I tried to tell your silly ass."

I tousle her hair, kissing her once more before heading to the bathroom. When I come back, she's tucked under the covers, watching my every move. Her deep skin is illuminated by the moon's reflection through the window.

I slide in beside her, pulling her closer to me. I kiss her neck, her cheek, and finally her lips.

"You are amazing, Mel," I tell her quietly. "In all ways."

We are silent for a moment, staring intensely at each other. A Rahsaan Patterson song plays softly in the background as she pulls me into a passionate kiss. And when our bodies meet again, I silently hope that all of her reservations about us will finally dissipate with the night.

I wake up to a warm body next to me and a strong arm wrapped around me. Tyrell is fast asleep in my bed, breathing steadily, looking so at peace. I shift slowly, careful not to disturb him, and slip out to grab my robe.

Last night was...incredible, to say the least. We had a great date and an even better nightcap. Ty was everything I knew he'd be, which somehow makes this more confusing. Yes, I like him. Hell yes, I'm attracted to him. It makes all the sense in the world for us to be together.

For some reason, though, what should feel right to me is currently feeling wrong, and I think about what my next move should be as I shower and get myself together.

Ty is still sleeping when I finish, and I decide the least I could do—before I tell him this can never happen again—is to make him some breakfast. I pull out eggs, chicken sausage, and some grits, set some music low on my Marshall speaker, and get to work. Cooking is a de-stressor for me. I tend to zone out while I'm in the middle of preparing a meal, the task becoming its own kind of escape.

I'm so caught up chopping onions and peppers, humming along to a Zhanè song, that I don't immediately notice the pair of eyes on me.

"Good morning, Kitty."

Tyrell appears before me, shirtless, wearing only his boxer briefs from last night.

"Morning, Sweetie. You see the things I left out for you?"

I left out a spare toothbrush and an oversized shirt and sweatpants I figured might fit him.

"Is that your way of checking whether or not I brushed my teeth before you kiss me?" he asks, eyebrow raised, smirk planted on his face.

He doesn't wait for an answer—just leans in, pressing a quick kiss on my lips. Then another, lingering a little longer this time, until I pull away. I'm not trying to start anything up again. Between last night, late last night, and early this morning, I barely got any rest, and I'd like to actually be productive today.

"You hungry? I'm making breakfast."

"Starving. I can't eat too much, though. I'm supposed to meet G and them at the gym for a training session."

I hide my disappointment, nodding as I get back to my chopping, not responding to the fact that he won't be staying long.

"Are we...going to talk about last night?"

He's leaning against my kitchen island now, arms crossed, neutral expression on his face.

I mirror it.

"What about last night?"

"Mel, don't make this complicated. Did you enjoy yourself? Can I take you out again soon?"

I pause my stirring to look up at him.

"You couldn't tell that I enjoyed myself? I thought I made that pretty obvious."

"Oh, I know you enjoyed *that*," he says, tucking a loose strand of hair behind my ear. "I'm talking about the actual date."

"I had a good time, Ty. I knew I would. You knew we would."

I turn away, focusing on plating our breakfast. I don't want to tell him I think we might've made a mistake. To be quite honest, I don't even know how to.

As if he's read my mind, he continues.

"I apologize if you feel like we moved too fast. I don't want you thinking I'm only interested in sex. You know that's not my intention at all."

"Don't apologize. I knew what I was doing before it was even a thought for you," I say lightly. "Trust me."

"Oh, so you planned to fuck me before I even had a say in it?"

He tousles my hair and retreats to the dining table just in time to avoid getting hit with the dish towel. I don't answer, but I know this won't be the last time he brings it up.

Tyrell is not a man who relies on context clues. He means exactly what he says, and he'll ask a question as many times as it takes to get a straight answer. He doesn't operate in gray areas.

I do.

My vulnerability issues keep me from letting personal matters be black and white. I know it's something I need to work on—I'm just not sure I'm ready. I'd rather walk around a difficult situation than navigate all the nuance required to get through it.

I place our plates down across from each other, Ty already seated by the window.

"I had a good time, you know," I say, taking my seat. "A really good time."

Maybe too good.

"I'm glad you did," he says easily. "It was the perfect date. I hope it's the first of many."

"Tyrell, I th-"

"One second, babe. Let me take this call."

His phone lights up with G's name.

"G! What up, bro?"

As he talks, eats, laughs, and pauses to wink at me, his energy fills the room. I decide that maybe today isn't the day to have a conversation about us. Maybe, I allow him and me to settle into this—this delusion that we can actually be more than friends—even if only for a little while.

When Ty hangs up, he turns his attention back to me.

"What were you trying to say earlier?"

"Nothing, Sweetie," I say, taking his hand, rubbing my thumb against his soft skin.

"You sure?"

His tone turns serious, but I assure him that it's nothing. We'll cross that bridge another day.

"Okay, then."

He finishes up his food, draining the last of his orange juice.

"I'm sorry to cut this short, but I gotta run."

"Yeah...of course."

I stand to walk him out, but he stops me in my tracks.

"Sit and relax. I know the way out. I'll send my house cleaner by later to take care of the dishes and whatever else you need done."

The thoughtfulness warms me, but I decline his offer.

"I'm good, but thank you."

He kisses my lips, slow and deliberate, like a promise he

wants me to remember. As he pulls away, his voice drops when he tells me he'll call me later.

I sit for a moment after he leaves, eyes closed, replaying the night and morning. When I open them, the flowers he bought catch my eye. I rush over, remembering the card he told me not to read yet.

I open it to a note in Ty's doctor-like handwriting.

Melody,

I hope our time together was everything you needed it to be and more. Thank you for always putting a smile on my face, as you've done so many times over the years. I plan to reciprocate those feelings every day, if you'll let me.

With adoration,
Tyrell
A song for you: Lalah Hathaway - "Angel"

A wide smile spreads across my face as I hold the card against my chest. I knew better than to fuck a jazz musician who sings and writes love songs. *Of course*, he has a way with words.

~

Later that evening, exhausted from running errands, I head to the mailroom to check for any PR packages. Among a few small boxes is a white Saks Fifth Avenue bag, folded shut so I can't see what's inside.

Back in my apartment, I rush to rip it open to reveal a red box trimmed in gold. Inside: a pair of gold René Caovilla wraparound sandals with a note inside.

> More to come.
> -Ty

I am absolutely, completely, and without a doubt, fucked.

I get to the studio on Monday evening around 5. Walking in, I see my uncle Keith, Tyrell, and our engineer, Dan, sitting at the soundboard. A few members of our band—Mike, Trevor, and Dave—are already here. I realize quickly that I'm the late one today, which is unusual because I'm always on time.

I have to admit, I was dragging my feet. I've been ducking Ty's calls and texts since yesterday, claiming to be busy or tired.

Be cool, Mel. You're a professional.

I am. And that's exactly why I haven't been able to speak to Ty. We crossed a line we shouldn't have—both professionally and as friends. Before we get in too deep, I have to do what I think is best for both of our careers. If that means putting some distance between us, then so be it.

The truth is, I regret having sex with him.

Don't get me wrong—to say that it was amazing would be an understatement. Our bodies connected in a way that felt magnetic, like they were bound together and couldn't be separated. We had a level of intimacy that's rare for two people touching each other for the first time. There was no learning curve. That man knew exactly what to do with my body.

The thought alone sends a rush of heat through me, but I shut it down quickly and remember where I'm at.

"Hey, Babygirl," my uncle greets as he stands up to hug me.

He's the reason I ever stepped into a studio to begin with. After my father passed away when I was eight, it was my uncle who introduced me to music as a way to heal through my grief. He stepped up when I needed a father figure, guiding me through a world I didn't yet understand. Over the years, he's worn every hat imaginable—songwriter, producer, vocalist, pianist, manager, musical director, mediator when Ty and I are on the brink of killing each other, and anything else I've needed.

His hug brings me back to my safe space.

"Hi, Uncle. I've missed you."

"I missed you, too, Princess," he says. "I'd miss you more, though, if you got your ass here on time."

I look up at him and laugh. He's never been one to beat around the bush.

"Mel! Good to see you," Dan calls out.

I make my rounds, hugging him and the rest of the band, keeping things light. Normal.

I feel Ty's eyes burning a hole through me before I even look at him. It's enough to make my shoulders tense.

"Hey, Kitty," he says as I step toward him.

I lean in for what turns into an awkward hug.

"Hey, Ty."

He pulls me in just a little closer, lowering his voice near my ear,

"I've been calling you. Everything good?"

The depth of his voice takes me back to the night he had me gripping the sheets, whispering obscenities in my ear as he dug his way through me. I pull away quickly, hoping he doesn't notice the way my body betrays me.

"Everything's good," I lie. "Ready to work?"

"Always," he says, flashing that familiar grin and punctuating it with a wink.

I don't return the smile.

I know immediately this is going to be harder than I thought.

We're at the studio on a Monday night, and Mel is being weird—there's no other way to describe it. She's barely acknowledging me, which somehow makes me want to talk to her even more. I chalk it up to her just trying to maintain her professionalism, but whatever she's doing is having the opposite effect. Her comments are short. The playfulness we usually have in the studio is gone. Even the tension we're known for is missing.

The last time we were here, Keith had to shut the session down early because we were close to cussing each other out. Tonight, I can barely get a full sentence out of her.

Interesting.

"Mel, I need you to come in a little higher on that last part," Uncle Keith says.

We're recording a new song that Mel wrote called *Ride*—a sensual mid-tempo track with minimal lyrics. I think it works better as an interlude leading into one of our slower songs. Mel wants to push it as a potential single. Another thing we disagree on.

"Yeah," I chime in. "I think it'll hit harder if you go up just a little more. We can layer the backgrounds to tie it together after."

"Right. Okay," she responds from the booth, already putting her headphones back on.

Dan restarts the track back over, and Mel nails it.

"How's that?"

"Perfect," I say. "Let's run the chorus again and fade it out with the instruments. Trev, give me a little more bass."

I'm trying to wrap this session up so I can talk to Mel. I have a feeling she's going to try to rush out of here the second we're done.

"Ty," Keith says, "go in the booth with Mel so we can clean up the chorus."

I head in. As soon as the door closes behind us, I place my hands on her waist. She stiffens, but she doesn't pull away. I lift her headphones just enough so she can hear me.

"You're avoiding me," I say quietly.

"Tyrell, we're working. Not now."

The firmness and clear annoyance in her voice only activates me. I lean into her back, hoping my touch will remind her she's safe with me.

"You can't avoid me forever," I whisper into her neck.

Unable to resist, she smiles back.

"Stop. Not here."

She puts her headphones back on, and I do the same.

Keith is staring at us through the glass, eyebrow raised.

"Y'all ready?"

We nod.

We run the chorus twice, then get a signal that we're good.

"Ight," Keith says. "Let's take a break before we get to the next song."

Mel moves fast, already halfway out of the booth. I follow her, grabbing a bottle of water, when Keith stops us.

"You two. Follow me."

Shit.

Mel and I quickly glance at each other, not saying a word. I'm silently praying that Keith just wants to talk to us about music. We barely make it outside before Keith turns around.

"How long y'all been fucking?"

Mel's eyes widen. I put my head down to avoid eye contact.

"Huh?" she asks, playing dumb.

"Don't 'huh' me," Keith snaps, mocking her in a high-pitched voice.

I laugh. Mel shoots me a cold glare that immediately sobers me.

"The last time we were here, I had to end the session early because y'all couldn't stop screaming at each other. Tonight, y'all in here whispering in each other's ears, giggling and shit. Y'all fuckin' around, and it's obvious."

I open my mouth, attempting to come up with a lie. "Ummmm..."

"It was only once!" Mel blurts.

"Twice," I correct. "Three times if you count the morning."

"TYRELL!" she squeals, hitting my arm.

"Melody," I shrug. No point in being modest now.

Fuck it. It's out in the open.

Keith throws his hands up.

"I don't believe this shit! Y'all had fifteen years to figure this out. Fifteen! Y'all go on podcasts denying your feelings, feeding the media this "we're just friends" bullshit, just for you to turn around and do exactly what they accuse you of doing."

He's not wrong. Every podcast, every interview—it feels like the public is in an uproar about our dating lives. I've even seen polls on gossip pages asking commenters if they think we're telling the truth about our relationship. We've done all we could to convince the world that our platonic relationship was strictly that. Going back on our word will only bring us unwanted press. We've worked too hard to have the focus shift from the music. I would never want our professionalism to be called into question.

"Look, we didn't intend for it to happen," I say. "It just did."

Keith sighs.

"Son, I was young once. I get it. You two spend a lot of time together, and I'm sure this was inevitable. But the timing is trash. Y'all horny asses couldn't wait?"

Leave it to Keith to give it to you straight.

Mel folds her arms.

"Yeah…well, it won't happen again."

I snap my head toward her. "Whoa. Let's not get carried away, now."

"And on that note," Keith says, already walking back inside, "I'm ordering some food. Y'all got ten minutes to figure this shit out."

Mel turns to me.

"He's right, Ty. We have to stop."

"Baby," I say, softening my voice, "we were just getting started."

She rolls her eyes. I take her hand in mine.

"We can be discreet, Mel. There's no reason to blow this up."

"There *is* a reason," she says, "if it compromises our career in any way. We've worked too hard to jeopardize that."

"Melody, I'm confused. What about us?" I ask. "Do we not also have real feelings for one another? Where do they fit in all of this?"

Unable to hide my annoyance at her dismissal, I drop her hand and take a step back, arms crossed. *This, I need to hear.*

"We don't even know *what* these feelings are," she says. "It was one date!"

"So that shit meant nothing to you, huh?" I ask.

She sighs heavily, and I can tell she's running from this conversation.

"I didn't say that."

"It's what it sounds like."

She gestures around us, frustration and something else etched across her face.

"What I'm saying is that we don't need to complicate everything for something that may not even be there. But this... this matters, Ty!"

"And so do you!" My voice tightens despite my effort to stay calm. "Are you really willing to ignore the possibility of a serious future with me? That seems kind of irrational and, honestly, unnecessary. It's fucked up, Mel."

I can see it land. The flicker of concession. She hears me, but her pride won't let her agree.

"I don't mean to sound fucked up," she says, measured, but defensive. "I'm just thinking about our careers. All the other shit can wait. This industry is brutal, especially for Black artists. There's not much longevity, and we still have groundwork to lay before we can afford distractions."

"So, we just pretend this didn't happen?" I ask. "I'm not saying you're wrong—but I don't see why we can't explore what this is *and* keep making music."

She knows I'm making a valid argument. I can tell by the way she exhales before answering.

"It's too risky, Tyrell. How are we going to keep people out of our business when you can't even keep your hands off of me in the studio?"

She has a point.

"The people in that studio are our friends and family," I

counter. "They know us. They don't give a fuck, as long as we're making good music and signing their checks."

"It's not *them* I'm worried about," she says sharply. "It's the media. Sponsors. Opportunities. Everything tied to our image and our income. You have to know when to turn that part of yourself off, and I don't know that you can."

Is she serious right now?

"Don't flatter yourself, Melody," I snap. "You're the one who could barely look at me all night. Ever consider that maybe *you're* the one who can't turn it off?"

Her mouth curves, but there's no humor in it.

"Yeah, well, maybe you're turning me off right now. How 'bout that?"

She turns to walk away. I follow.

"Here you go with the petty shit."

"Fuck off, Ty," she fires back. "We need to get back to work."

"Fuck that. Don't think this conversation's over either."

She stops abruptly, turning back to me with a smile that unsettles me—too calm, too final.

"I hope you enjoyed this while it lasted. Conversation done."

I watch her walk back inside, jaw tight, chest heavy. She's right about one thing—I can't be touching her like that in the studio. I'll have to tighten up. Be more careful. Maintain my professionalism.

But that doesn't erase what I'm feeling.

This conversation isn't finished. It's just been postponed.

And one way or another, Mel and I are going to deal with this.

Tonight.

After the conversation outside, the rest of our studio session goes fine enough. We're as professional as we can be—keeping our distance, only talking when necessary. I know he's pissed at me, but it's for the best. He'll thank me later.

We wrap around 8:30, and I say my goodbyes before heading to my car. I haven't even been on the road for three minutes when my phone rings.

Tyrell.

Here we go.

"Yes, Tyrell Hampton. How can I help you?"

"So formal," he says. "Is this your version of professionalism?"

"Surely you have better things to do than run your mouth on my phone. How can I help you?"

"We need to have a real conversation, Mel. Actually talk through this."

We do—but not in person. I don't trust either of us like that right now.

"You talking me through things is how we ended up in this situation to begin with."

"See, I wasn't even trying to go there," he replies. "But I see that's where your mind is. I'll come by your spot, and we'll talk face-to-face. I'm serious."

He sounds serious. And that's exactly the problem.

Truthfully, I'm not ready to expose my feelings. The other night, I was more vulnerable than I usually allow myself to be. I can't even blame it on the liquor—the two little cocktails I had at dinner were long gone by the time we got to my place. The real problem is how comfortable I felt with Ty. How easy it was.

Sounds like a silly thing to complain about, but when vulnerability is not your strength outside of putting it in your music, feelings become difficult to sort through.

I trust Ty completely, but I'm afraid of the unknown. What if it doesn't work out between us? What if everything we've built—professionally and personally—gets compromised? Ty has been one of my closest friends for fifteen years. Losing that would wreck me. It's a risk I'm not sure I'm willing to take.

I need to communicate this to him.

"I believe you," I tell him. "Come by when you can."

"Bet. Be there in thirty."

Thirty minutes pass before I hear it—the knock that mirrors my heartbeat. I open the door to see Ty standing there—locs pulled up in a bun, hazel eyes glistening, flowers in hand.

"Hey, Kitty."

His smile is shy. His voice, easy. It does something to me.

I arch a curious brow. "How did you even get into my building?"

He smiles —slow, unapologetic. "You really think a little door was gonna stop me?"

Swoon.

Then, quieter, more real, "Groundskeeper was coming in. I got lucky."

He lifts the flowers. "These are for you," he says. "I'm sorry for earlier. Even though you started it."

I laugh, despite myself. "Thank you. Where did you even find flowers this time of night?"

"Trader Joe's," he says proudly. "Did you know they close at nine? I had to race there before they closed."

"That's very sweet of you. I appreciate the peace offering."

I hug him, and the embrace lingers longer than it should. I take in his scent, catching the familiar trace of his Bond No.9 cologne. *He always smells so good...*

I'm getting distracted, and this is exactly why I didn't want him here.

"You're welcome, baby," he says quietly. "I don't want to fight. I just want to get this right. Feel me?"

I pull away to look at him. "I feel you. And I'm sorry I was a bitch earlier."

"Just a little bit of a bitch," he replies, smirking. "Not that much."

And just like that, we are back to being ourselves.

I walk into the kitchen, smelling my flowers along the way, looking for a vase to put them in.

"Do you want something to drink?"

"Water," he calls out. "And a glass of wine."

Of course.

When I come back, he's already made himself comfortable —shoes off, jacket gone, flipping through channels like he lives here. I sit across from him, deliberately choosing the chair instead of the couch.

He notices me as I settle into my seat.

"You can't even handle sitting next to me," he says with a grin. "Good to know I have that effect on you."

"Boy, please," I reply, sipping my wine. "I'm just giving you space since you've made yourself so comfortable on *my* couch."

He studies me for a moment, then drops the teasing.

"Do you like me, Mel?"

Straight to it.

"You couldn't even ease into that?"

"Last I recall, you don't need any easing."

I ignore the commentary. "I do like you, Ty. I never said I didn't. I'm curious—but I won't pretend it doesn't feel risky."

He nods, taking another sip of wine. "You're right. All I'm saying is that we should at least try. What's wrong with us really dating? Getting to know each other in that way?"

"Because if we get caught, people will think we lied," I say. "I don't want to be seen as a liar in the court of public opinion. I don't want our fans to feel played. We have a very small niche and are gaining a loyal fan base. Trust matters."

"We won't get caught," he says calmly. "We'll be careful. Date openly in small towns or in areas where people won't know or care who we are. We'll keep it professional in the studio and otherwise. Friendly, but appropriate."

"No touching," I add. "Nothing that contradicts what we tell people."

Ty smiles deviously. "Deal."

"I don't trust that smile, Ty."

"What's the worst that could happen between us, Mel? Seriously?"

I hesitate. "Ummm. What if we stop speaking? What if it gets so messy we can't come back from it?"

His posture shifts. Serious now.

"Whatever happens between us, we handle it with respect... privately. I would never intentionally hurt you. You have my word."

I exhale. "I can live with that. So...where do we start?" He closes the distance, takes my hand, and pulls me up, guiding me onto the couch—onto him.

"We can start here."

His lips brush my neck. Soft. Unrushed.

I tilt my head back and laugh, breathless. "I thought you wanted to get to know each other?"

"This *is* getting to know each other," he mutters, lifting the hem of my shirt.

We are absolutely fucked.

"I thought you said I couldn't fuck you again," I say against her skin. "Look at you taking all this dick like my good Kitty."

Her response isn't words—it's the way her body reacts, the way she arches into me like instinct has taken over where logic failed. Every sound she makes pulls something deeper out of me, something I've been trying not to name since the first time we crossed this line.

My breath is uneven as I pin Mel down, stroking in and out, controlled only by the rhythm we fall into together. I want her to feel every second, to understand exactly what she does to me without me having to say it.

"Mmmmm, right there, baby. You feel so good."

Her sweet voice is intoxicating, her moans sending vibrations through me. This is the best sex I've had in a while, and it's wild that it's with my best friend. I don't even know if we can call each other that anymore. I don't know what we are, officially. I just know that I love being inside of her.

I pick up my pace slightly, knowing it will send her over the edge. I stay right there with her, refusing to let the moment pass too quickly, watching the way her composure melts the longer I hold her there.

When her body finally gives in—shaking, as her orgasm erupts—it's beautiful. I kiss her neck like I'm anchoring us both to something real, and make my way down to the piercing on her left nipple.

"Come here," she says, pulling my face up to meet hers, eyes searching mine like she's trying to read everything I'm not saying out loud. She holds my face in her hand, kissing me sweetly.

My speed slows down as I take her hand in mine, continuing to stroke her. I kiss her again, taking in all her beauty.

I'm so glad she's mine.

CHAPTER 26
Tyrell

July 2012

It's the summer after my sophomore year of college, my first completed year at USC. I managed to land an internship at an accounting firm for the summer, which means I'm gone for most of the day, usually making it back home in time for dinner with my grandma.

Four years ago, my mother passed away from a heart attack, leaving my family and me completely devastated. My mother, Anne, was an amazing woman, but she worked a lot to make ends meet. As a single parent without even a high school diploma, she worked two jobs to take care of my sister, Tia, and me, but was often burnt out. The stress of raising two children while living in the hood and trying to keep us out of trouble—still trying to maintain her own life, all while chasing my sister's cheating-ass daddy all around LA—weighed heavily on her.

When she passed away, my sister opted to live with her aunt on her dad's side. My only option was to live with my grandmother since I didn't know who my father was. I've been living with my grandmother in Compton for four years now, trying to hold my grief together for her sake while picking up the pieces in the process.

Today is an especially hard day for me because today is my mother's birthday. Though I am grateful for the woman that she was while she was here, I can't help but miss her deeply. I feel a mix of emotions today, mainly anger. My mother didn't deserve to die from what I now know was stress at the young age of forty-five. She deserved a life of peace, leisure, and rest—and she never got to experience any of it.

While she was alive, I always promised her that I was going to put us in a position where she didn't have to work so hard anymore. The pain of not being able to make good on that promise while she was alive still haunts me.

"Boy, get inside and stop letting all my cool air out!" My grandmother's thunderous voice calls as I stand in the doorway, checking the mailbox.

I love my grandma, and I know today is a hard day for her, too, but I'm not in the mood for her nagging about every little thing.

"You had a lot of mail in that box, Nana," I say, after taking off my bag and shoes, dropping the mail on the entryway counter. I'm eager to get out of my work clothes, shower, and relax. Maybe even smoke a blunt once Nana goes to sleep to take my mind off my mom.

"That ain't nothing but bills and nonsense. It can wait. Come sit with me for a minute."

She pats the seat next to her on the plastic-covered sofa.

"You know today's your mama's birthday," she says softly, eyes glistening.

"How could I forget? I miss my girl."

My heart feels heavy, and I try not to show it. One of us has to be strong. My grandmother had to bury her only daughter, then turn around and raise a teenage grandson. She shouldn't have to be the strong one here.

"I miss her too," she says. "But I know she's damn proud of you. She would be so happy to see what you've done with your life. And you know I'm proud of you, too."

I take my grandmother's soft, wrinkled hands in mine—hands that tell the story of a woman who lived a hard life and did the best she could with what she had. Hands that sacrificed and labored so I could have the opportunities that weren't afforded to her or my mother.

"Thank you, Nana. That means a lot to me."

We sit in silence for a moment before a smile creeps across her face.

"I baked a cake for your mama. Reach in that top drawer and get the candles out."

"Chocolate cake?"

"You know it! That girl loved her some sweets. I'd bake a cake on a Sunday evening, and Anne about ate the whole thing by Monday morning."

We laugh at the memory of my mother's affinity for sweets, something she definitely passed down to me. Every birthday while she was alive, my grandmother made her a three-layer vanilla cake with chocolate frosting. We'd crowd around the old espresso-brown wooden dining table, my mother seated in front of her cake with four candles...always four. She'd still be in her post office uniform, hair pulled back in a tight ponytail, black-rimmed glasses on, eyes closed tight as she blew out the candles.

After her passing, my grandmother and I made a tradition of blowing out the four candles, each of us saying a silent prayer. Mine is always the same: that my mother is resting well, that she is at peace, and that she continues to watch over me, as

I do my best to make her proud. It's a simple prayer, but it feels fitting for my Anne, who was a simple woman.

As we eat our slices of cake with nothing but *Wheel of Fortune* playing softly in the background, my grandmother breaks her silence.

"Melody called earlier, you know. She asked for you to call her when you could."

"Oh yeah? I'll call her a little later then."

Mel knows this is a hard day for me. Once I shared with her last week that my mother's birthday was coming up, she became extra attentive—calling me in the mornings before I leave for my internship, stopping by some nights just to check on me.

We've talked on my grandmother's house phone almost every night since the semester ended, sometimes meeting up on the weekends to chill at her uncle's spot or on the front porch here. All of my internship money is going toward next year's tuition, so I haven't had the money to go out, party, or travel like some of my homies. Mel doesn't seem to mind, though.

"She's a pretty little thing, Tyrell," Nana says. "I don't see why you don't just go steady with her."

I laugh at that. Since I introduced her to my college friends, Melody is the one my grandmother talks about the most. I swear she loves that girl more than she loves me.

"Nana, you know it's not like that between us. We're just good friends. That's all it is, and that's all it's going to be."

"Says who?" Her voice rises as she peers at me over her glasses.

"Says her. Says both of us, really. We have a lot in common, and she's a good friend to me. Nothing more, nothing less."

My grandmother waves her hand dismissively.

"Boy, you 'bout as blind as a bat if you don't see how much

that girl likes you! She's been on my front porch just about every Saturday to see about you."

"Nana, Melody would tell you herself that there's nothing between us. She's a good person. She cares about me, I know that. I care about her too. But all that extra stuff you're talking about? It's not happening."

She pauses a moment, then fixes me with a knowing look.

"Listen to me good, Tyrell. I might be old, but I know a thing or two. Don't be blind to what's right in front of you. Melody is good for you, and you're good for her."

I chuckle, shaking my head at my grandmother's relentlessness. I do have a soft spot for Melody. Truth is, I'd probably be with her in an instant if she ever said she had real feelings for me. But she's content with us being friends, so I don't have much choice but to be content with that, too.

"I'll keep that in mind, Nana," I say, smiling at my grandmother.

"Mark my words. It'll happen someday."

Days after the studio session earlier this week, I wake up to the sound of my phone chiming back-to-back, alerting me that I've received multiple text messages.

I have an interview scheduled today with *Vivid* magazine, a men's-focused publication that features popular male visual and performing artists. I was selected to appear in an article highlighting up-and-coming musicians. I planned to wake up early this morning to prepare—but not 7:03 a.m. early.

I forgot to put my phone on Do Not Disturb last night and immediately regret the decision.

Most of the messages are coming from the group chat I'm in with my boys from college. They don't usually text this early, so something must be going on. Whatever it is, I know it better be worth the sleep I'm losing.

I scroll up to the beginning of the messages, my eyes widening when I see the screenshots of Melody and me—from the night we were out at Dirty on 85, and from the night of our first date.

My stomach drops.

I had no idea we were being watched.

Now, we've been posted on every major Black media outlet, with headlines like: **"More Than Just Friends? R&B Duo 'Mel & Ty' Spotted Getting Extra Close"**

"Fuck!" I shout, throwing my covers back.

This is exactly the situation Mel and I were trying to avoid.

Almost immediately, guilt settles in. I'm the one who got extra close to her. I'm the one who initiated the date. The screenshots don't help my case at all—Mel and I standing too close at the lounge, me whispering in her ear, my face inches from hers like I'm about to kiss her. Her hand in mine at dinner. My arm wrapped around her waist as I led her out of a restaurant.

Damn.

I brace myself and start reading the messages in the chat, knowing whatever commentary my bros have is probably worse than the comment section on those posts.

> G
>
> Woke up to see Mel & Ty finally decided to fuck with each other after 15 years. I called this shit.
>
> KEV
>
> That nigga Ty is whipped. Been whipped, actually.
>
> BRIAN
>
> He's been in love with her since we were like 18, 19. Nigga definitely played the long game lol.
>
> G
>
> Watch they still deny that they deal with each other.
>
> BRIAN
>
> Which one y'all think started this up?

KEV

Definitely not Melody's ass. She been
curving Ty since we were sophomores. I
guess he finally wore her down lol.

G

Mel's gonna lose her shit when she sees
this. You know she hates any publicity that
ain't about the music.

BRIAN

It's her fault! Both of their faults, actually.
Why niggas thought they could go on
dates and shit and not be seen is beyond
me lol.

KEV

Lol you know they about to spin it and say
it was just business.

G

That shit ain't even believable. They look
like a seasoned couple lmao.

BRIAN

Fasho look like they been together for
years lol.

G

Niggas probably live together and never
even told us.

BRIAN

Niggas probably eloped and never even
told us lol.

KEV

I wouldn't put it past them. I never saw two
people more in love deny it for so long.

First off, fuck y'all niggas.

G

😂😂😂

                              Mel and I are just cool. Y'all know that.

BRIAN

This nigga.

KEV

Me and Kim cool too. I don't take her out
on dates tho and hold her hand and shit.

G

Ty, you hit that yet???

                                        Watch it, nigga.

KEV

Yoooooo 😂😂😂

BRIAN

😂😂😂😂😂

G

😂😂😂😂😂😂

                                  Man, fuck y'all LOL

G

They're working thru their shit. This is new
territory. 😂

KEV

Yeah, this nigga Ty fasho in love.

BRIAN

Ty, idk why you and Mel keep denying shit.
In all seriousness, y'all belong together.

              On some real shit, it's Mel. She thinks it's
              bad for business.

G

BRIAN

KEV

I toss my phone onto the bed, feeling a mix of annoyance, aggravation—and unexpectedly—relief.

Getting caught is the complete opposite of what Mel and I wanted. And I hate people knowing my business before I get a chance to tell it myself. But there's another side to this: if people already think we're together, part of me wonders if we might as well be.

I personally don't care about the public's perception of Melody and me. I know the truth. I know the timeline. And I have no problem being honest. The truth is, we finally decided to act on our feelings. Whether those feelings were always there isn't anyone's business but ours.

What *does* matter right now is Mel.

She tried to shut things down at the studio, and I was pretty sure I gave her enough dick that night to temporarily forget about that. Clearly, that didn't last long, because she's back to ducking me outside of work shit.

I know she's seen the posts by now.

And knowing Melody, the attention has definitely made her even more uncomfortable. I already know how this goes—public scrutiny makes her retreat, not lean in.

I scroll through the comments. Most people are saying that they knew we were secretly together. Some are questioning why we'd lie in the first place. A few joke that our music is so good *because* we're sleeping together.

Then I see the ugly ones.

Comments implying that Mel slept with me to get me to write and produce music for her. Wondering who else she slept with to get noticed in the industry.

My jaw tightens.

That couldn't be further from the truth. Melody worked extremely hard to get to where she is. She'd never use her body for leverage. She wants her talent to speak—always has. That's why she stays quiet online, never engages the bullshit, never feeds the noise.

I know those comments would hurt her if she saw them.

I decide not to bring this up today. She's probably already processing enough. This can be a conversation for another time.

I am seated across from my interviewer, Logan Chanel, waiting to get started.

I was given a rundown of topics beforehand—how Mel and I met, how our business relationship developed, my background as a pianist, and my creative process. Standard stuff. The interview is going well...until it isn't.

Logan: You and Melody seem incredibly in sync creatively.

Do you think there's a personal aspect there that contributes to that chemistry?

Me: Well, as many people know, Mel and I have been friends for fifteen years. We've also worked together for fifteen years. We've had time to learn each other's styles in terms of writing, producing, and ideation. At this point, our process is seamless because we've had years to refine it.

Logan: And that shows. As listeners, though, so much of your music explores love, relationships, sex, and all of the intricacies that make-or-break intimate relationships. I'm going to ask this question on behalf of all of your fans who want to know—are you singing about each other?

I laugh, more to hide my discomfort than anything else.

Me: I draw inspiration from so many things—my own experiences, things I've witnessed people close to me go through, even ideals of what I want in a relationship. Melody *has* been the subject of a couple of songs...but I'm not saying which ones.

We both laugh, and I hope this is the end of that line of questioning.

Logan: I'll take that as a yes. The chemistry between you two is obviously there and reflects in your music. I think many of us are just surprised that things between you two haven't turned into more.

I sigh, choosing my words carefully.

Me: Mel and I built a really strong friendship over the years. She's been there for me at my lowest, and I've supported her too. What people call chemistry is really just familiarity. She's like my work wife.

Logan: I don't think that's helping your case. You know how many men cheat with their work wives?

I laugh—hard.

Me: I can't even say you're lying because that type of thing happens all the time. But as of now, Melody and I are just friends. Those lines haven't been blurred...at least not yet.

It's a lie.

But it's one the world doesn't need to know yet.

Logan: "Not yet" means there's a chance. As a fan, I'm rooting for you both!

We both chuckle, then wrap the interview talking about music, influences, and the future of R&B and Jazz.

It's Thursday evening, and I've been avoiding my social media pages for most of the day, not wanting to see articles of Ty and me on full display. I definitely don't want to read the comments about us.

After the mess earlier this week—which brought questions from every single friend of mine, my grandmother, and extended family, plus a firm lecture from Uncle Keith—I'm completely over it. I knew this was a bad idea, yet I let all logic fly out the window. I'm used to thinking with my head, but this time I thought with my heart instead, and got involved in a situation with Ty that isn't easy to get out of.

It doesn't help that I haven't really spoken to him much. Every time Ty's called this past week, I've lied and said I was in the middle of something and would call him back. When he texts, I wait hours to respond—long enough to know he's probably already asleep.

I feel bad about avoiding him because I know I'm being ridiculous and incredibly immature. I'm just not ready to confront my feelings for him. I really, really, *really*, like Ty. And not just because he's been an amazing friend, but because he truly is a gentleman. He's intentional. He's gentle. He's consistent. We connect on every level. He's been everything I've needed and wanted.

But pushing him away is easier than dealing with emotions.

I'd like to say that prior to last year, I was much more open to falling in love and being with one person. I've had my share of lovers and heartbreak—relationships with men that ended in cheating or quiet separations, always picking up the pieces and starting over again. I never gave up on love...until my last interaction with my mother.

After my father's death years ago, my mother blamed me for the reason she and my dad got into the car that night in the first place. She turned to alcohol and spent years neglecting me in an attempt to erase her own guilt and grieve him the way she felt she needed to. Once I became an adult, she only reached out to me when she needed money.

Last year, I tried one final time to get her to go to rehab. She cursed me out, made me feel horrible, and told me to leave her the fuck alone. The very next day, she texted asking for money. When I refused to fund her addiction, she cursed me out again.

So, I blocked her.

I never told anyone why I decided to go no-contact with my mother, and it's been killing me to carry that alone. I'm not someone who brings my problems to others. I keep my feelings bottled up, reserved just for me to sort through—if I ever do.

The pain of realizing that I have no parental support from my only living biological parent hit me like a ton of bricks. Since then, I've been extra cautious about letting people in. My priorities shifted to nurturing the relationships that actually show up for me. I had to grieve my mother privately—not because she died, but because I know we'll never have the relationship that I've desired for the last twenty-six years.

I can't afford to lose another person that I love so deeply.

So, I do what I know how to do best: I control the risk. I push Ty to the side, ignore my feelings, and pretend they don't —or never did—exist.

And yet.

Despite what my brain keeps telling me, I can't stop replaying Ty and I's first official date. I catch myself smiling at memories of staying up all night trying to get a melody right for a song we never even planned to release. The more I avoid him, the more I think about him. And the more I think about him, the more I want him—mentally, emotionally, and damn sure physically.

Flashbacks of him in my bed, in control but still affectionate, cloud my thoughts.

The only thing that pulls me from the memory of Ty's dick inside of me is the sound of Logan Chanel's voice on my screen, asking Ty if there's a personal reason our chemistry is so strong.

I roll my eyes, then keep watching.

I'm usually the one who gets asked these questions, so I'm curious to see how Ty answers—especially now that we've actually crossed that line. He doesn't give away much verbally, but his smile, his demeanor...they say enough. When Logan asks about our status, he says the lines haven't been blurred *yet*.

I'm slightly annoyed with his response, especially since we've already spent days in headlines.

But I can't lie—I'm flattered.

Even though I've been ducking him and trying to end whatever this is, he's still leaving space for us.

~

My publicist and manager, Jaime, loves her 9 a.m. meetings. Normally, that wouldn't be an issue for me—I've been an early bird since I was six. I remember waking up at seven on weekends, running into my parents' room with my missing teeth and cartoon pajamas, bouncing onto their king-sized bed.

Mom was always agitated by my early morning enthusiasm. Daddy, on the other hand, never complained.

He used to say it was good that I liked waking up before everyone else.

I carried that habit with me my whole life—except today.

I tossed and turned all night, barely sleeping, my mind stuck on Tyrell. After my appearance on the *On A High Note* podcast and Ty's *Vivid* interview, the online chatter about us denying our relationship exploded. Everyone told me not to read the comments.

That lasted about ten minutes.

People accused us of lying for attention. Of being swingers. They even accused me of sleeping my way to the top. Absolute bullshit. If anyone knows how to fix this, it's Jaime—manager, publicist, and therapist all in one. That's why I'm here.

I walk into her office in a monochrome navy-blue look— wide-leg trousers, silk top, patent leather slingbacks, hair slicked into a low bun. If nothing else, I want to look better than I feel, which is like absolute shit.

"Come in!" Jaime's chipper voice greets me.

She pulls me into a hug, looking chic in her all-black attire. "Mel! How are you, honey?"

"I've been better," I admit, sinking into the chair across from her desk. "I don't know what to do about this thing with Tyrell. It's stressing me out."

"You two looked awfully close in those pictures, Melody," she says gently. "But you know the media. You'll be a hot topic for a week max, and then things will die down. The next story is always more interesting than the last."

Maybe I am overreacting—but I hate *this* being the reason we're talked about.

"What do you think we should do?" I ask. "I need your expertise."

"That depends," Jaime says. "Are you two planning to move forward with a relationship? Is this serious?"

"No," I answer quickly. "We went out a couple of times, but I don't think getting serious is a good idea. I've told him that."

Jaime raises an eyebrow, and I know follow-up questions are on the way.

"And how does Tyrell feel about it?"

"I'm not sure that he agrees. But I think this is best for our careers."

Jaime hums. "Well, if it's casual...why not be seen with other people? Maybe you both need to date others to take the heat off of whatever you have going on."

My eyes widen. I don't think it's a terrible idea, but I don't think it's a good idea either.

"Do you think people will buy that?"

"People will buy whatever you sell them, Mel," she continues. "If you want to present as a single woman, you have to do what single women do. Date. Let people see that you're both interested in other people."

I consider Jaime's words, thinking about what dating in the spotlight would even look like for Tyrell and me. I've been so focused on getting our career off the ground that I haven't really thought about my personal life or dating at all. Before my first date with Tyrell, I hadn't had sex in almost a year.

Now that things were looking up for us, I guess I should think about optics a little more. How can I deny to people that

I'm not caught up with this man if I'm only ever seen out with him? Maybe Jaime does have a point.

"Maybe you're right, J," I say slowly. "I need to find someone to date, though."

"Oh my God, that reminds me!" Jaime squeals, and her excitement is contagious enough that I find myself smiling, despite everything.

"What are you so giddy about?"

"Victor Washington asked me about you last week. I completely forgot to tell you. I'm sure he'd be a good distraction from Tyrell."

"Fine ass, acting ass, Victor Washington???" I ask, eyes stretching.

"Yes! He's my client now, too. He knows I work with you and Tyrell, and he asked if I could introduce you two or pass your number along."

Victor Washington is an upcoming A-list actor and model, steadily gaining more visibility after landing a major Broadway role a few years ago. He moved to LA earlier this year and is set to star in a highly anticipated Netflix series soon.

"I don't know about that, Jaime..." I say, already feeling conflicted.

"Oh, stop, Mel. Victor is a sweetheart. You two would probably really hit it off. I'll pass him your number and suggest he take you to Nobu. Someone is *always* recording celebrities coming in and out of that place—so I'm sure you'll be noticed by at least one person."

"Well..." I hesitate, then nod. "Okay. I hope this works."

Jaime and I move on to talking about upcoming appearances, new music, and brand partnerships. But even as the conversation shifts, my mind stays right where it was.

Because while dating someone else might be a good idea for the brand, it doesn't feel like it's the *right* option. Don't get me wrong—I don't think Tyrell and I should be together. But that doesn't mean I want him involved with anyone else.

And if I'm being completely honest?

I don't want to be with anyone else either.

I sigh deeply, the music turned off as I drive home after the meeting, sitting alone in my thoughts. I just hope I'm making the right decision.

CHAPTER 29

Tyrell

My phone rings at 8:17 p.m., and I'm surprised to see Melody's name across my screen. Her disappearing act over the last week has left me confused as hell, so I'm curious about what she's calling for now. I don't give myself time to come up with a game plan before I answer, eager to hear her voice.

If only this woman knew the *effect* she has on me.

"Melody," I say. "To whom do I owe the pleasure?"

"Hello to you too, Tyrell. How are you?"

There's a rasp in her voice that tells me that she's lying down, and my mind immediately fills in the blanks—her sprawled out on her bed, glasses on, little to no clothing on...

"Better now. How are you?" I pause, then add, "I miss you."

I can't even make it ten seconds without wearing my heart on my sleeve. *A fucking fool.*

"I miss you too. *Really*. But I called to talk to you about something."

She takes a deep breath, and my stomach tightens. Whenever Mel takes a breath like that, it's never good news—never something that works out in my favor.

"I'm all ears," I say, trying to sound supportive.

"Well...I met with Jaime earlier today to talk about what's been going on with us in the media. I know you always tell me not to read the comments, but I did. And it's bothering me. Jaime suggested that we...date other people."

"What?!" I sit up. "Why?"

"She thinks it'll take the heat off people assuming you and I are together. She brought up the fact that I've been single since we blew up, but haven't been spotted out with anyone but you. Jaime says people might need to see us both with new faces so they know we're not together. I'm hoping this puts the focus back on our music and not our personal lives."

"Oh," I say sharply, "so you agree with that bullshit?"

I try to play it cool, but there is no scenario where I'm okay with the woman that I want dating another man. I can't believe Mel is even entertaining this.

"Ty...it's not going to be anything serious. Just a few dates until things die down."

"So, you're okay with me dating other women?" I ask. "Because I'm not okay with you dating other men."

"You're single, babe. I can't tell you what you can and can't do. I don't love this idea either, but I think it's the best option for us right now."

She sighs, and I know her well enough to know her mind is already made up.

"Where does this leave us, Mel?" I ask. "I haven't heard from you all week. Every time I try to talk to you about a future, you shut me down."

"Ty, I told you that I don't think you and I are a good idea right now—and you know why. Look at what's happening. People are more worried about whether or not we're fucking than they are about our art. That was always my biggest concern, and now we're seeing it play out. I—I don't think we should've crossed that line. And I don't think we should cross it again."

I lean my head back against the couch cushion, staring up at the ceiling, trying to process what she just said.

I understand her concerns. I really do. But, fuck that! These people don't know us, and they're not entitled to our personal lives. I don't understand why she can't just tune out the noise.

"So that's it then, huh?" I ask. "Just like that? You didn't even give us a fair chance."

"I can't give us a fair chance," she says quietly. "Not right now, at least."

I let out a humorless laugh. "You know what? I don't even know why I expected a different response from you. Before we were even caught in public, you were already trying to get rid of me. I'm sure this wasn't even Jaime's idea."

"It wasn't m-"

"It's cool, Mel," I cut in. "I hear you."

There's a pause, heavy and unresolved.

"I'll see you at the studio on Thursday."

I hang up before she can respond.

I can't keep chasing a woman who has no desire to be chosen out loud. If this is what she wants—distance, denial, pretending—then that's exactly what she's going to get.

My phone lights up with an incoming call, and an unknown number scrolls across the screen.

"Hello?" I answer cautiously.

"Hi, Melody. This is Victor Washington."

Shit. I didn't think he'd actually call.

"Hey Victor. How are you?"

I try to sound warm—pleasant, even. After my conversation with Tyrell last night (which he ended very abruptly, by the way), I've been having second thoughts about this whole plan to date other people. From the outside looking in, it probably seems innocent enough—the kind of thing celebrities do all the time. And while Tyrell and I are nowhere near mainstream, we wouldn't be the first people to date for the sake of sending a message.

PR relationships happen so often that it's hard to tell who's in love and who's just cosplaying it for their image. Victor and I could easily be another Hollywood fling that people pay attention to for a moment and then forget about. That was what I wanted to explain to Tyrell before he shut the conversation down. He sounded so hurt by the suggestion that I almost feel guilty even answering this call.

"I'm doing well," Victor says. "Much better now that I've finally gotten a hold of you. You're kind of a hard person to reach, Melody."

His voice is a deep baritone, but his tone is easy, light, and affable.

"Well, you can blame Jaime for that," I counter. "She delivered your message to me about a week late."

"It's okay," he laughs. "I was willing to wait however long it took just to talk to you...So I could ask you out on a date."

Oh, he's smooth.

"I'm flattered," I admit. "But we don't even know each other. How do you know you'd even want to go out with me when we haven't had a real conversation yet?"

I'd be lying if I said my curiosity wasn't growing by the minute. There's no harm in hearing him out...right?

"Your interviews tell me a lot about you," he says. "You're smart, passionate about your work, and incredibly talented. And it doesn't hurt that you're absolutely beautiful. I don't think I need to be sold any further."

A smile creeps onto my face, and I know my tone gives me away when I respond.

"And what did you have in mind for this hypothetical date?"

"Well, first, I'd love to take you to dinner. Jaime told me you're a fan of Nobu, so I thought we could start there. After that, maybe a private tasting at a cocktail bar owned by a friend of mine. I'm open to whatever you'd enjoy. Being in your presence would be enough, honestly."

"You have a way with words, Mr. Washington."

I try not to let on that he's already convinced me, but I think it might be a little too late for that.

"Can I take you on a date this Saturday, Melody?" he asks. "Let me show you *exactly* how good I am with my words."

Victor's confidence is nothing short of rousing, and is a quality that I love in a man. A man who is sure of himself and secure in who he is will always be a major turn-on for me.

I agree to the date with Victor.

We work out all of the details, then chat a little before we eventually hang up. To my surprise, Victor isn't nearly as self-absorbed as I expected a handsome, up-and-coming actor to be.

Now comes the hard part.

Tyrell.

I bite my lip, staring at my phone, then finally decide to text him.

> Hey. You still mad at me?

TY

> You know I can't stay mad at you for too long. You were talking some bullshit, though.

> Okay first off, this was not my plan. It was completely Jaime's idea. And you have to admit that it makes a little sense, Tyrell.

TY

> I don't have to admit shit. Humor me though—how does it make sense for two people who like each other and want to be together to date other people?

I pause before I respond, knowing my next messages won't go over well.

It's not that easy. You've read the
comments on those blog posts. Being
rumored together right now is taking the
focus off of our talent and all of the work
that we're putting in. People care more
about our relationship status than our
music. We've worked way too hard for that.

I hesitate, but continue.

Let's just go out on a few dates with other
people until things die down. It's not
serious. You know that.

TY

You can try to dress it up however you
want, Mel...I still don't like it.

You're going real hard about this. You must
already have some shit lined up.

I won't lie...I do. But it's one date. It
doesn't mean anything.

TY

At this point, fuck it. Enjoy yourself.

My intention isn't to hurt you, Ty. I hope you
know that.

TY

That's the thing about intentions. They
don't always match the impact.

It's cool, Mel. Do you. Have a good night.

"Fuck."

I toss my phone onto the couch and lean back in my chair,
exhaling deeply. I hate this. I hate hurting Tyrell. I hate even
being in this situation.

But I keep telling myself it's for the best—for both our careers and my heart.

Whether or not he wants to see it that way isn't up to me.

Putting distance between Tyrell and me is going to have to be the new norm. I just have to trust that, eventually, this will all make sense.

Tonight is my date with Victor Washington.

For the last few days, our conversations have been good. He's kind, attentive, complimentary—an overall sweetheart. Despite him being absolutely perfect so far, I'm dreading this date. If I'm being honest with myself, Tyrell is the reason why.

Truthfully, I don't want to be with anyone else. I don't want to date anyone else. Even though this date with Victor might be what's best for my image and my career, it's the complete opposite of what I actually want—which is to be with Tyrell.

As I apply my lipstick, I remind myself that this is for the best. If Tyrell and I aren't together, we can't hurt each other permanently. I would rather give up what *could be* and keep him as my business partner and friend, than take a risk on love that could cost me him entirely.

I tell myself this will all be worth it in the end.

They say, *If you can't be with the one you love, love the one you're with.* I guess that will have to be my motto moving forward.

Victor picks me up at my apartment, and we head over to Nobu—which I'm sure is packed tonight. The ride over is smooth. He jokes, tells me stories about his family and upbringing, and I try my best to stay present as he recounts a funny memory involving his sister from when they were kids.

I do my best to block out thoughts of Tyrell.

As uninterested as I claim to be in this date—or this man—I have to admit that Victor is very charming and easy to talk to. Even with my mind elsewhere, the conversation flows naturally. Before I know it, we're pulling up to the valet, and Victor is helping me out of the car.

As he guides me inside, I take a deep breath and brace myself for the night.

You can do this. It's just dinner.

I give myself a quick pep talk as we follow the hostess to our table. I catch a few whispers as we move through the restaurant—mostly about Victor.

At least this plan is working.

Victor takes the seat across from me, smiling as our waiter places menus on the table.

"I love the food here."

"I can tell," I tease. "Your eyes lit up when we got the menus. I'm ready to see how you look once the food actually arrives."

We laugh easily, the conversation flowing to our favorite restaurants in LA and other cities we've visited. Things feel light—comfortable—until Victor's expression changes slightly, and the tone shifts.

"So...I hope I'm not overstepping when I ask this," he says.

I raise an eyebrow. "I'm sure you're not. Ask away."

"I saw the pictures of you and Tyrell," he says. "I know the media tends to exaggerate things, so I wanted to ask you for myself. What's going on with you two?"

His expression is more stoic now—genuinely curious. I keep my own face neutral, careful not to give anything away.

"Tyrell and I go out as friends from time to time," I say evenly. "Nothing more, nothing less. We've been friends for years, so we're closer than most people realize."

I surprise myself with how easily the lie rolls off my tongue.

Victor smirks slightly, and I can't tell if he really buys it or not.

"Hmm," he says. "Okay. Fair enough. Did you know he'd be here tonight?"

My stomach drops.

"What?" I pause, trying to be mindful of my reaction.

Victor nods subtly towards the restaurant entrance.

"Tyrell's here," he says. "And he's walking toward our table."

I turn my head—

—and there he is.

Tyrell.

With Natalie.

Walking straight towards us.

CHAPTER 32

Tyrell

Outside of business obligations, I didn't talk to Mel for a few days after our phone conversation. The speech she gave me about us needing to date other people annoyed the shit out of me, and I wasn't in the mood to talk to her—or about her.

Natalie called me out of the blue the other day to check on me, and I have to admit, hearing the warmth in her tone was a welcoming distraction from my feelings toward Melody. Though I didn't feel sparks with Natalie, I did feel wanted—desired, even. It was a welcome shift from my recent interactions with Mel, which more often than not had left me feeling the complete opposite.

When Natalie suggested that we get together this weekend, I offered to take her to one of her favorite restaurants—Nobu. I figured if Mel was going to date, me taking Natalie out wouldn't hurt.

When Natalie and I entered the restaurant, I immediately noticed Victor Washington seated in a booth across from a woman with a familiar set of big curls.

Is that...Melody?

I couldn't see her face clearly enough to confirm it. Before I jumped to conclusions, I decided to walk over and say hello. Though Victor and I had never met in person, we shared the same management and followed each other on social media. Taking Natalie by the hand, I walked towards the table.

The moment the woman turned around, my stomach dropped.

Melody.

I felt my face harden instantly before I forced myself to fix it. Still, not before giving her a quick look I knew she'd interpret as *what the fuck are you doing here?!* She smiled at Natalie, polite and composed, then shot that same glare back to me—as if to say, *I should be asking you that!*

I extend my hand to Victor as he stands from the booth.

"Tyrell! It's good to finally meet you, man."

"Good to meet you too," I reply. "Figured we'd run into each other sooner than later. This is Natalie."

Natalie greets Melody and Victor warmly, immediately engaging Victor in small talk about some of his roles that she loved. I take advantage of the distraction, pulling Melody into a brief hug.

"What the fuck, Mel?!" I whisper into her ear.

"You have a lot of nerve," she whispers back.

We pull apart, both of us carefully rearranging our faces into something pleasant. I laugh as she sits back down, and she does the same, as if we've shared some private joke.

Bullshit.

The four of us exchange pleasantries, talking about the dishes that we love at the restaurant. I ask Victor about his drink, doing my best to stay neutral. After a few minutes, I wish them a good night, shaking Victor's hand.

I lean in to kiss Mel on the cheek.

The look between us says everything we can't.

Natalie and I are conveniently seated nearby.

Great.

I tell myself to be cool as I take my seat—unfortunately positioned with a direct line of sight to Melody. I would laugh at how ridiculous this situation is if it didn't piss me off so much. All of this could've been avoided if she'd just stop running from what's clearly between us.

"Babe, did you hear what I said?"

Natalie's tap on my hand pulls me back from the woman across the room.

"I'm sorry," I say quickly. "What did you say?"

"I said Victor invited us to the advanced screening of his new show. I told him we'd love to support him."

"Oh, right. Yeah," I reply. "That's cool."

My tone is more nonchalant than it should be, but fuck it. I don't give a fuck about Victor or any show that he has coming out. Not when I'm watching him take Melody's hand in his.

Before I can even react, the waiter arrives to take our orders. Once that's done, Natalie excuses herself to go to the restroom.

I lock my attention on Melody.

The servers have just brought out their food. I watch as Victor feeds Melody sticky rice and salmon tartare, like this is some intimate little moment meant just for them.

This is some bullshit.

She laughs, opening her mouth slowly, flicking her tongue in a seductive way that has me ready to flip this table over. Her eyes meet mine—and she has the audacity to wink at me.

It takes everything in me to calm myself down.

It's just one date, I remind myself.

Just one.

And two can play that game.

I wink back just as Natalie returns to the table. I take her hand, lifting it to my lips and pressing a kiss there, making sure it's visible.

I don't need to look to know that Melody's watching...

I feel it.

Let the games begin.

CHAPTER 33

Melody

This nigga.

I don't believe this shit. After Tyrell gave me so much attitude the other day about following Jaime's plan, he has the audacity to be out with Natalie—*of all people!* I would've at least felt better if it were someone new. The fact that she and Tyrell have history makes their being together tonight feel like a personal attack. The way he's sitting there, acting interested in what she's saying, kissing her hand, and showing all thirty-two of his teeth as he smiles at her is slowly making my blood boil.

But like he said the other day—*fuck it.*

He's a grown man.

He's a *single* man.

He can technically date whoever he wants.

The duality of that thought is that, as a woman in the same position, I can also date and do whoever *I* want.

I decide to stop giving Tyrell the pleasure of my attention. I don't need him knowing how upset this situation is making me. If he wants to play up this little date he's on with Natalie, I'm going to do the same. And I'm going to do it better.

Victor has his eyes locked on the dessert menu.

"What are you in the mood for?" he asks.

I drop my voice down to a low rasp. "Chocolate. Dark chocolate, actually."

His eyes lift to mine, lust-filled and unmistakably intentional. Victor licks his lips, then takes a slow sip of his drink.

"Funny," he says. "I'm in the mood for the same."

His deep brown skin echoes the tone of my own, and I quickly realize that this man is not a novice at flirting and enticing women. I laugh at his response and pretend to refocus on the dessert menu as the waiter approaches.

Victor orders the only chocolate-infused dessert on the menu and another round of drinks. As soon as the waiter leaves, my eyes betray me, drifting right back to Natalie and Tyrell.

It seems like they're having their own moment, as Natalie leans across the table to whisper something into Tyrell's ear. He smiles, slow and deliberate, and then—like he *feels* me watching—his eyes find mine.

"Yeah," he says, loud enough for me to hear. "I'd like that a lot."

Fuck him. And fuck Natalie's thirsty ass too.

I know he's doing this on purpose. Saying whatever he thinks is going to make me the most jealous. And the fucked up part?

It's working.

I excuse myself to the restroom, locking myself inside a stall and closing my eyes as I exhale. *Just breathe. This is not worth losing your composure over.*

My Zen moment is interrupted by a text on my phone.

My heart rate spikes when I see Tyrell's name.

I type back immediately.

The response comes fast.

I don't respond...because I can't.

Tyrell is absolutely right, and there's no way that I can deny that.

Playing this game with him is only making things worse. For me. For us.

When I leave the restroom, I decide that I'm going to be mature about this and stop forcing something that doesn't exist. Victor doesn't deserve to be collateral damage in whatever unresolved mess Tyrell and I are in.

I return to the table just as the server sets down our dessert and drinks. Victor's smile widens when he sees me.

"Are you smiling at me," I ask, picking up my spoon, "or at the desserts?"

"I was just watching you walk back from the restroom," he

says. "You know, about five men nearly broke their necks to look at you."

I laugh. "You are such a liar. Those men weren't paying me any mind."

Victor scoops up a bite of the dessert and lifts it to my mouth.

"Or maybe," he says softly, "you just don't realize how incredibly beautiful you are, Melody."

His words make me melt a little, and I have to look away for a second to keep him from noticing. It's hard not to stare at him, though. That beautiful, smooth, sun-kissed skin is addicting to look at, and I'm sure it would be even better to taste.

And for a fleeting second, I'm tempted to flirt my way into Victor's bed.

A revenge fuck. A distraction.

But I know it's not the right or smart thing to do.

I immediately regret the flirting. Am I attracted to the fine ass man sitting across from me? Absolutely. But was I attracted to him enough to compromise whatever Tyrell and I have?

No.

Because when I lie down at night, it's Tyrell I think about. It's Tyrell I want to share my highs and lows with. The one I want to create with, laugh with, and just do life with. Even now —especially now—it's him.

Victor doesn't deserve to be a pawn in this game. And fucking him tonight won't give me the post-nut clarity I'm pretending I need.

Victor pays the bill and helps me out of my seat, his hands settling around my waist. Before I can process what's happening, I feel his lips brush mine—soft, confident, public.

The room spins.

And then I see it.

Tyrell's face.

The deep scowl. The tension. The hurt he's trying—and failing—to hide.

Victor takes my hand and leads me toward the exit. I glance back once more, catching Tyrell's eyes.

The frown that he's wearing nearly breaks me.

CHAPTER 34

Tyrell

I'm furious.

Melody calls me about this "date other people" plan, then admits to already having a date lined up. I end up lining something up too, in an attempt to make myself feel better about this plan. Somehow, Melody and I end up on dates at the same restaurant, and I just had to watch her date feed her, kiss her, and leave with her. I don't even want to imagine what the end of their night is going to look like. The thought of Victor sliding his dick in and out of *my* girl has me in such a rage, I barely even notice when Natalie asks,

"You okay? You look like something's bothering you."

"Yeah, I'm straight. Kinda ready to get out of here."

I take a long sip of the glass of Uncle Nearest I've been drinking, as I notice Natalie's angelic face staring at me intensely.

Through my rage, I can't help but smile a little at the woman sitting across from me.

"You know, when you look at me like that," I say, "I start to think you really want me."

"I *do* really want you, Tyrell. It's hard for me to look at you any other way."

As I take Natalie's hand in mine, I remind myself that this is a woman who truly likes me and isn't afraid to move forward. She isn't hindered by a past or by her fears. All she wants to do is share her affection with me. I've been fighting to win the affection of a woman who just left a restaurant hand-in-hand with another man, and for what? And yeah, maybe I don't feel that spark or passion with Natalie that I feel with Melody. But could I learn to?

"Are you all done with your food? If so, I'll get the bill so we can head out."

"You don't want to see the dessert menu?" Natalie questions, knowing it's completely unlike me to resist ordering sweets after a great meal.

I smirk at her after I get our waiter's attention.

"I have other plans for dessert."

I am quiet as I walk Natalie inside her apartment.

Quiet as she removes my shirt first, running her fingers down the length of my chest and stomach until she reaches my pants. I am even quiet as I remove her dress, the bareness of all of her camel-toned skin coming into view.

I am quiet because when I kissed Natalie for the first time in a long time, it felt...wrong. And though my body now reacts to her touch, her smell, and the beauty she possesses, my mind is elsewhere.

I pretend well enough as I glide in and out of her, hoping she doesn't notice how distracted I truly am.

In the moment, it felt right to take Natalie home and make

love to her, justifying it with the assumption that Melody was probably on her way to do the same thing with Victor.

But when she looked into my eyes before she turned to walk out with him, I swear I saw a twinge of guilt in her expression, and maybe even a hint of regret. It's almost as if Melody knew that we both had gone too far. It's almost as if she was quietly admitting to me that we had both made a mistake.

It's all I keep thinking about and replaying in my mind, even as Natalie calls my name, traces her fingers across my back, begging me not to stop. I follow her commands, seeing her pleasure through as I feel the drip of her release.

When I look down at her passion-engrossed face, I close my eyes tight.

And envision Melody's face instead as I find my own release.

CHAPTER 35

Melody

May 2014
Senior Year

I t's the night before graduation, and I'm tired, tipsy, and unbearably hot in a dorm stuffed to capacity with seniors. It's tradition to stay up the night before graduation, drink to the point of oblivion, then turn getting to commencement on time into an Olympic sport. I hadn't planned on participating, but my girls guilt-tripped me, insisting this might be the last night we'd all be together before reality set in and life took over.

Tisha and Sydney are taking shots with classmates from their senior seminar, barely noticing when I announce that I'm stepping outside to get some air. I maneuver my way out of the dorm, grateful for the cool breeze that hits my skin the second I step outside the dormitory. As I head toward a bench along the side of the building, I catch the shadow of a familiar stride approaching.

"What you doing outside by yourself, Mel?"

Tyrell's voice is unmistakable.

"It's hot as hell in that dorm. I had to come get some air."

"Damn, then maybe I shouldn't go in," he says, sitting next to me. "I just came from the shit Jay and them were throwing in Cardinal Gardens. Everybody was drunk except me."

"You're not drinking tonight?" I ask. "It's tradition."

Tyrell opens this jacket, revealing a pint of Hennessy tucked inside the interior pocket. We both laugh as he pulls it out and offers me some. I take it, shaking my head.

"This is probably a bad idea, but fuck it."

"Our last drinks as undergrads," he says. "You nervous about graduating?"

His hand covers mine as he helps twist the cap open.

"Yes and no. I'm ready to start this master's program so I can get it over with. But I really wanna try with the music. I think we can actually make something happen."

We've talked about starting a music group countless times. Written dozens of songs. Played open mics. Entertained friends at kickbacks. It's always lived somewhere between a dream and a hobby.

"It costs money to record, Mel," Tyrell says. "Studio time, paying the band, engineers, all that shit. I'm not rich like you and your little boyfriend, you know. I need time to get my shit together."

"Okay, first of all, Nate is *not* my boyfriend," I say firmly. "He's moving to London, and neither of us is committed enough to try to make long-distance work. It was fun while it lasted, though."

Tyrell takes the bottle back, taking a swig, then focuses his eyes on me.

"So, you're back on the market now?"

That smile. The one he uses when he's flirting with purpose. "Depends on who's asking," I say lightly, poking the dimple in his right cheek.

Tyrell hasn't tried to get with me since sophomore year when we first met. After I denied him for the second time, we eased into a friendship because of our proximity as music minors. If he's asking about my relationship status now, I assume it's because one of his friends is trying to get at me.

He copies my gesture, using his index finger to touch my own dimple.

"I'm asking."

The seriousness of his tone, mixed with the emphasis on *I'm,* startles me, and a confused look settles on my face.

"You can't be *that* drunk," I say, attempting to casually laugh it off.

"Drunk words reveal sober thoughts, you know."

He nudges me with one arm, forcing our bodies closer.

"Ha! You know damn well you're not interested in me. We friend-zoned each other a long time ago."

"No," Tyrell counters. "You friend-zoned *me*. I just never pushed the issue." He pauses, looking at me.

"Doesn't mean I don't think about it."

His gaze is steady but earnest, and it keeps me from looking away.

"I can't even imagine us as more than friends. We might kill each other," I say, grabbing the bottle from him and taking another shot. I don't think I'm drunk enough for this conversation.

"So, you're telling me you've never thought about us dating?" he chuckles. "I find that very hard to believe."

"Um, I don't know why that would be hard to believe. I'm not on your dick like every other girl on this campus."

"I'm not stupid, Mel. I see the way you look at me. The way you work overtime to tuck that jealousy whenever you find out I'm dealing with someone new. You treat me better than you've treated guys you were dating, and it's not just because you want to be a good friend."

"Ty, you are delu-"

"Let me finish." His voice is calm, but certain. "We've been friends for a while. We'll probably be cool for the rest of our lives. But one day, we're both going to stop lying to ourselves about what this really is."

"Oh, you are *definitely* drunk," I say. "Because that's never going to happen."

I roll my eyes, keeping my face neutral, feigning disinterest.

But the truth is—Ty is...right.

On more than one occasion, I've looked at him and thought, *what if?*

I think about the nights we stayed up late working on midterms and finals for our music classes, him sitting at his piano, acting as my accompanist while I sang. The times I'd write songs and immediately rush to find him, because I knew only he could instantly put a melody to my words. Those moments we locked eyes, once we realized the moment our creativity had just...clicked.

His fingers over mine as he tried to teach me how to play piano, guiding me patiently. His hand on my back whenever I felt frustrated and wanted to quit. Me calling or texting him about every minor inconvenience of my day. Bringing back leftovers whenever I went home for the weekend because I knew he loved my uncle's cooking.

There have been so many small moments over the years where I've questioned whether Ty and I could be more than just friends. Just as quickly as those thoughts came, I made a habit of forcing them back down, reminding myself that risking our friendship with complicated feelings was not worth it. Not to mention—Ty is a hot commodity on campus and off. I never wanted to be caught in the trap of being one of his many.

"Never say never," he says, winking as I playfully push him away.

"Remember we had this conversation twenty years from now when we're married."

We both laugh at that, and he slips an arm around me. We sit in silence for a moment, staring out in the same direction, the weight and uncertainty of what's to come as new graduates settling in around us.

"Uh huh," I say, leaning my head on his shoulder. "I'll remember every word."

CHAPTER 36

Melody

I t's the night of our performance on Anderson West's Late Night Show, and Tyrell and I are barely even speaking.

After we spent our entire Saturday evening at dinner recently trying to make each other jealous by overly flirting with our dates, we haven't spoken about anything unrelated to business since. Our usual banter is nonexistent. We've barely had two words to say to each other, aside from "Good Morning" and "Goodnight." I recall the look on Tyrell's face that night before I left the restaurant with Victor, and it immediately dampens my mood. The anger and hurt that his expression revealed in that moment made me realize that this isn't the way I wanted things to be between us.

I told Victor that I wasn't feeling well and shut down any plans he had to visit a cocktail bar and possibly have a nightcap. When I got back home, I was tempted to text Tyrell and tell him I thought we both made a mistake, but I didn't have the words. Frustrated with both myself and Tyrell, I've been sitting with these emotions for two weeks now, still unsure of how to proceed with things.

Tonight's live performance is the most important of our career thus far, and the excitement for it (at least, from my point of view) has been diminished because I currently can't stand the man I'm sharing this moment with. I normally would be calling him every spare second I had, or sitting in his apartment working out last-minute kinks in our performance. It's our first time on television, and neither one of us seems even remotely interested in trying to fix the personal issues between us.

We've rehearsed for this performance five times in the last couple of weeks, and yet every time I look at Tyrell, I battle with the desire to cuss him out, punch him in his face, or invite him over to my place and fuck him until the sun comes up.

I'd be lying if I said I didn't miss his touch. More than that, though, I miss his friendship. I miss our jokes. I miss the comfort that his presence brings me on stage. The only thing between us on stage right now is tension, which is the very thing I was afraid of happening.

My face must be giving away exactly how I feel.

"You okay, Mel? You look out of it." My makeup artist sprays the final layer of finishing spray on my face, and her expression is curious as she continues talking.

"You don't seem like yourself, hon."

"I'm fine." I force a quiet laugh out. "Just a little nervous. This is a big deal, you know?!"

"I get it. Just relax. You're a professional, and you were born for this. And you have Tyrell on stage with you, thankfully, so only half of the attention is on you.

Thankfully, my ass. I do my best not to scoff at the mention of his name in response. I can't for the life of me understand why he would villainize me for wanting us to temporarily date other people, then immediately be out with someone he has no business dealing with. And okay, maybe I don't have the right to be that mad. But what the fuck?! I'm mad as hell.

The more I think about it, the more heat rises to the top of my skin. I realize quickly that I need to calm myself down before I get on that stage, and fast.

Someone from production pops in to give us a five-minute warning, and I emerge from my seat to gaze into the closest full-length mirror. *At least I look good,* I tell myself, as I take a series of deep breaths. As soon as my eyes open, Tyrell comes into my line of vision, head peeking into the dressing room.

His eyes slowly move up and down my body, which is dressed in a brown leather skirt and matching corset, styled with brown knee-high boots.

"You ready, Melody?" The sound of his deep voice immediately makes my insides tingle, but I mentally shake those feelings off and give him a quick nod in response. We're performing a new song that Ty and I wrote together, *"Losing Time."* It's the next single releasing from our upcoming album, and is a mid-tempo song about two lovers putting their differences aside amidst conflict to remind themselves that they love one another. Ironically, the song represents the exact space that Ty and I *should* be in, but neither one of us wants to start the conversation. The song is sexy and has some light choreography that requires Ty and me to be a lot closer than either of us probably wants to be at this point. I try to remember that I'm an artist and entertainer first and foremost.

Production gestures for us to enter the hallway before we're announced to the stage.

"You okay?" Ty leans over to ask.

"I'm good." My response is short, and since I know Ty, I already know where this is about to head.

"This is all because of you, you know. That attitude you have should be directed at yourself."

"Now's not the time for this, Tyrell."

"It's never the time for this, according to you, Melody."

We are glaring at each other, eyebrows tight, frowns planted on our faces. Neither one of us looks like we're ready for a performance of this magnitude. I turn my head from the heat of Tyrell's glare and focus on what's in front of me: the performance that could propel our career, the art that I care so deeply about, and the music that I've worked on tirelessly with this man to create.

We are led to the stage to get in position, and I quickly try to snap out of the foul mood Tyrell just put me in. I pass Uncle Keith as I make my way to the mic stand positioned for me, and his comforting smile immediately calms me.

I need to remember why I'm here, I remind myself. *This is not about our personal drama. This is about our music.*

The sound of Anderson West's voice rings loud through the speaker as I focus on the magnitude of people in the audience.

"This next group has been making a lot of waves with their viral, sultry hit song, '*Tonight*.' Here to perform "Losing Time" from their highly anticipated debut album, *For the Lover In You*, please welcome for the first time to our show— Mel & Ty!"

The audience erupts into applause, and the band begins their brief introduction, followed by Ty starting his verse. Although he sounds exactly how he did in rehearsals and his voice is strong and beautiful, I can immediately tell from his disposition that he's not himself. I sing my parts, trying to remember the choreography and sell it as much as I can. Part of the choreography called for us to touch one another, which both of us seem to be avoiding at the moment. It feels awkward and somewhat forced when our bodies do eventually connect. As I'm singing this sexy song that hints at the physical making up lovers might do after a confrontation, I feel like I'm only going through the motions. Despite my pep talk to myself, my mind is completely distracted. The passion I usually have on stage is nowhere to be found.

We finish the song as best as we both seemingly can, and the audience erupts in applause. *Maybe it wasn't that bad,* I say to myself. Yeah, we might have sounded great, but I know in my heart that the performance we just put on was not nearly as great as it could've been.

As we exit the stage, I am disappointed in myself, mostly for how I allowed personal feelings to take me off my game. I'm just hoping that no one else picked up on Tyrell and I's lackluster energy.

When I stepped off the stage the other night, I knew immediately that neither Mel nor I had given our all. We let our personal issues bleed into the performance. Instead of focusing on the magnitude of the opportunity in front of us, we moved like two people who didn't even want to be there.

The reaction to our performance doesn't surprise me as I scroll through comments on Instagram, X, and Threads.

BigApple98: Why do Mel & Ty look like they just got done cussing each other out before they went on stage?

ThatGuySparks007: They sound 'ight. But them niggas look like they'd rather be anywhere but on stage together.

MizFitMayhem2000: Not too much on my girl, Mel. They both sound amazing. But something is definitely...off.

User12098374657349216664: I hope this doesn't mean that they're going to stop making music together. They didn't even put their album out yet and already can't get along.

User95304593020: This is exactly why you're not supposed to shit where you eat.

ThatGuySparks007: Yeah, those "dates" at Nobu were fake ass news. Not gonna lie tho, Mel is fine as fuck. I would've tried to get at her too.

MrsMakeItNasty112: Tyrell baby, call me. I promise I can put you in a much better mood.

I lock my phone and let it fall onto the bed beside me.

I guess Mel was right after all.

I stare up at the ceiling, replaying everything in my head. We only went out a couple of times, and already our emotions have thrown us completely off our game. That scares me more than I want to admit. Not because of what it means for the music—but because of what it means for us.

I don't want to believe she was right about us being a bad idea. I don't want to accept that something that feels this real could be this disruptive. But the evidence is right there, playing back in real time for the whole world to see.

I can't dwell on this, though.

I need to fix this ASAP. Not just for business, but for personal reasons too. Mel and I can't function—professionally or personally—with this kind of tension hanging between us.

I don't know exactly how I'm going to do it yet.

I just know I can't let things stay like this.

CHAPTER 38

Tyrell

The phone rings twice before Mel's uncle, Keith, picks up.

"Hey, Unc. How you feeling?"

"I'm alright. Can't complain. What's up, Nephew?"

"Need to run something by you. Can I stop by?"

"I'm home all day. Come through."

"Bet. Be there an hour."

I head west on I-10 toward Unc's beach house in Malibu, my thoughts heavy. This situation with Melody has had me in a bad headspace, and Unc is one of the few men I trust to give me sound advice. He's a man of peace who rarely gets out of character, and both he and his home always reflect that. The panoramic ocean views from his living room don't hurt, either.

I pull into Unc's expansive driveway and ring the doorbell.

"You look like shit, Nephew," he says after one glance at me.

Uncle Keith isn't one for warm welcomes, but he isn't lying either. I haven't been sleeping well. I feel like I'm Tom, and Melody is my Jerry, chasing her endlessly with no sign of winning in sight. It doesn't help that I haven't shaved in a couple of weeks either.

I ignore the insult, dap him up, and step inside, kicking off my sneakers.

"It's been one of those days, Unc."

"We've all been there. Drink?"

"Whiskey on the rocks."

Keith raises an eyebrow, surprised by my straight, no-chaser request.

"Sir Davis?"

"You know it."

Unc pulls the bottle from his extensive collection and fills two glasses with ice.

"You drinking too?"

"A man shouldn't drink alone when he's in distress."

Damn, I must look worse than I thought.

"I never said I was in distress, Unc. I said I needed to run something by you."

"Let me guess," he says dryly. "The something has to do with my niece?"

"This situation is really fucking with me, Unc." I take the glass from him and take a long sip. "She's all over the place."

"This is a tough position for both of you. The heart and the mind being at odds is never good for the spirit."

I nod in agreement. "I really care about Melody. I came here to vent, but also to be clear about my intentions. If she and I can figure this out, I'm all in."

I pause, trying to gather my next thoughts.

"I want you to know that I can take care of her. Protect her. Provide. I fully intend to marry her...hopefully with your agreement, Unc."

Keith sits across from me at his dining table, poker face on. He takes a sip of his drink, and I fully expect him to either cuss me out or kick my ass. Instead, he sets the glass down and smiles.

"Oh, she really fucked you up, huh?" He laughs, shaking his head. "You have my blessing, Ty. Nothing you're saying surprises me, though."

"You knew?!" I ask.

"I knew from the year Melody brought all her college friends over for the holidays that you two had a thing, whether you admitted it or not. I might not have said much, but I'm very perceptive."

"But she was in a relationship at the time. Swore she was in love with Mike." I chuckle, remembering her college boyfriend. He talked a good game, convinced her eighteen-year-old ass that they were getting married after graduation, then got caught cheating. She never looked back.

Unc continues, "I watched the way she interacted with all of her male friends, and how you moved around the women in that group. With everyone else, things were strictly platonic. With you two, it was different. The looks when you thought no one was watching. The way she would lock eyes with you, smile, and look away. I could always tell there was something there. You two always put on a good act, especially when you brought dates around. But you can't fool a nigga like me, though."

Unc is clearly amused by this situation. The casual way he speaks about Mel and me puts me at ease, however, and I relax a bit.

"I'm not even gonna lie. When I first met Mel, I tried to get at her even though I had a girl and she was with Mike. Thought I could wear her down. I chased her for two weeks before realizing she was dead serious. After that, we kept running into each other around campus and realized we had a lot in common, especially when it came to music. The friendship just took off."

"Well, Mel is easy to love," Unc says. "I obviously don't have to sell you on that, though."

He cracks up, and I feel slightly exposed.

"Unc, I'm being serious here. I don't know what to do! One day, she wants to be together. The next, she avoids me completely. I can't understand her."

"That's not new to me. I raised her."

"How do I fix this?" The urgency in my voice surprises even me.

"Well, first off, understand this: the feelings are mutual. She likes you just as much as you like her. A fool could see that."

"Then why the games?"

"Mel has always been logical. Somewhere in that brain of hers, she thinks it's safer for you two to walk away with your friendship and feelings intact than to risk things blowing up completely."

"I would never feel that way about her, Unc."

"You two spend a lot of time together. Career-wise, romantically, physically. That kind of dependence can take a toll."

"I don't see a downside to being with someone I know this well."

"Familiarity breeds contempt."

I sit with that.

Maybe Melody *is* just trying to be logical. Maybe she'd rather protect the music and the friendship than risk everything collapsing at once. We're both passionate people. Trying to balance love and ambition wouldn't be easy.

"You're right," I finally say. "So where do I go from here?"

"You and Melody have a communication problem. There's a reason you're here talking to me and not my niece."

"You're not wrong. It's rough when we argue. Melody's mouth is crazy when she gets upset."

"Shiiiit, don't I know it? I had to walk out of the house a few times when she was a teenager to calm myself down. She has her ways, just like we all do."

"It's funny because she's still the sweetest woman I've ever met. She'd give anybody the shirt off her back."

"Then cuss you out right after for needing a shirt in the first place."

We both laugh at this, and something softens in my chest. *This is why I'm in love with her.*

In love with her?!

The thought rattles me. I take another sip of my drink.

"You and Melody spend more time talking at each other than you do listening to each other," Unc says, snapping me out of my thoughts.

"I can agree with that. She's the only woman I know who can get under my skin."

"Ty, you know I love you like my own," he says, his tone shifting. "So, I don't mean no harm with what I'm about to say..."

"I appreciate you saying that," I respond. "You're the only real male figure I have in my life."

"And I don't take that lightly. It's not my intention to throw your past back in your face, but I know what happened with Kimora."

I nod.

That relationship wasn't my proudest moment, and I've spent the last few years working on myself because of it. Though Kimora and I did come to love one another, our relationship started as a one-night stand that quickly turned into us being inseparable. She moved in not long after, and for a while, things felt intense in a good way.

But just as quickly as we fell in love, the relationship shifted.

There was a lack of trust on her end, and a desire for us to move to the next level, fast—marriage, kids, the whole picture. At the time, I didn't feel like we were there yet. Instead of talking through it, we argued. A lot. What started as disagreements at home escalated into raised voices, then into arguments in public. It got ugly.

The final straw came when Kimora showed up at my job one day to start an argument with me because I hadn't answered my phone. That was the moment I knew I had to end it. Pulling away from her was incredibly hard, but necessary. We brought out the worst in each other, and by the end of it, I left mentally and emotionally drained. I drank more than I ever had before. After going through that with her, I knew I never wanted that to be my reality again—especially not with Melody.

Unc continues, "When it comes to you and Melody, I'm not getting involved in your relationship nonsense. Disagreements, issues, cheating—whatever it is—I'm not in that shit. But when you and her get into it and you feel yourself getting close to that point, you walk away. My niece is not sitting in a toxic situation that affects her mental health. If you think you're about to drag her through that, think again. And if you ever introduce her to a hostile relationship, I won't hesitate to put my Glock to your throat. And you know I'm not bull-shitting."

I am taken back by his words, but I don't take them as disrespect. This is a man being a protector. Melody went through a lot with her mom last year. She puts on a tough exterior, but she's vulnerable right now. I would never want to put her in a situation where we're constantly arguing or calling each other out of our names. She deserves peace and respect—not the bullshit Kimora and I had.

"I wouldn't expect anything less from you," I say. "I respect it. But I would never do that to her."

"Oh, I know you wouldn't try me like that," Unc says, laughing. "And Mel would probably kick your ass before I got to you."

I laugh. "True. I'm not proud of how things went down with Kimora. Every time I run into her, I apologize. I've felt bad for years. That shit had me in therapy twice."

"It's all a part of life, nephew," Unc says. "The highs, the lows. You take them as they come and evolve."

"Man, I remember the first relationship I got into after Kimora. That was when I was with Courtney."

"I remember Courtney. Melody couldn't stand her ass."

"Ha! Eventually, I came to see why. The first six or so months were easy, almost too easy. To the point where I started picking little fights just to feel something. I had to unpack that shit. My therapist told me that I was so used to the toxicity from my relationship with Kimora, chaos became my norm."

He nods. "And I see the growth. Rarely do I even hear you raise your voice—except when it comes to Melody."

"That woman knows how to push my buttons," I admit. "You see us go back and forth in the studio, but most times we call each other after and apologize. I can't stay mad at her for too long."

Unc gives me a teasing grin. "That's because you're in love with her."

I can't deny it if I tried...and so, I don't.

"I'm finally admitting that to myself."

"The next person you need to admit it to is Melody."

The suggestion makes my stomach twist.

"I don't want to scare her off. She's already avoiding me."

"I'm not saying she's right for how she's handling things," Unc says. "But I know my niece. She's acting out of fear. She wouldn't be this scared of losing you if she wasn't in love with you, too."

Memories of Melody flood my mind—years of moments, conversations, laughter, music. I can't deny the truth in his words.

"Life is short," he continues. "Real love is rare. You and Mel have something special. I say, lay it all out on the table. Even if she rejects it, you can know that as a man, you were honest with yourself and her. It's easier to live with the outcome when you know you did all you could."

"You're right about that, Unc. You got a lot of relationship advice for a single man."

"It's much easier to give advice than to take it," he says with a sheepish grin. "I'm working on something, though."

"Awwww, shit. Who is she?" Now it's my turn to tease him about *his* love life.

"Stay outta grown folk business."

We laugh, shoot pool, drink, and watch sports in the basement until it's time for me to head out.

As I'm leaving, I thank him for his wisdom. "I appreciate you talking to me about all this. It's been weighing on me for a minute."

"Anytime, nephew. I meant what I said earlier. You're family. You know you can call me whenever."

Rarely do Keith and I hug, but it seems fitting for the moment. I'm grateful to have the wisdom of a man I admire, blood or not.

"Love you, Nephew."

"Love you, Unc."

As I drive back down I-10 to Hollywood Hills, I replay everything Keith said.

I know exactly what I need to do.

Tonight is Sydney's birthday dinner. Unfortunately—or maybe not—it's also a night that requires me to be in the same space as Tyrell for something that isn't work-ordained.

Tyrell and I haven't really been speaking since the whole Nobu situation. We had one studio session last week that was quick and void of any real conversation. We showed up, did the work, and left. No jokes. No lingering. No effort to pretend that things were okay.

We appeared at a brand-sponsored event together, taking pictures with big smiles meant to fool the world into believing that we're a cohesive unit both in music and in real life. Dinner at the event was awkward, especially since we were obviously seated next to one another. We exchanged surface-level small talk while I spent most of the evening talking with a popular influencer beside me. We made conversation with others who recognized us and helped lighten the tension by telling us how much they loved our music.

Ty, who has always been the more reserved of us two in social settings, seemed slightly out of place for some of the evening. Thankfully for us both, he quickly bonded with an influencer's husband over sports and spent the rest of the night talking about teams, stats, and seasons. From the outside looking in, we probably looked like two people who complemented one another effortlessly.

The truth is, beyond pleasantries, words escaped us both.

Tyrell walked me to my car afterward, saying very little. The perplexed look on his face said more than he probably wanted it to. I knew he wanted to say more than the "Goodnight" he offered before turning away. I wanted to say more too, but at that moment—and honestly, at any moment that night—I couldn't find the words.

Now, I'm standing in my closet, rummaging through hangers, trying to find something to wear to impress a man I've been actively avoiding.

And not because I hate him. Not because I don't care.

Because I still don't know what to say.

Yes, I have deep feelings for Tyrell. That's the truth I keep circling back to. But it never should've gotten this far. Everyone knows the advice against not shitting where you eat, and yet Tyrell and I ignored it completely. Now, we've made a mess of things.

I want to be with him, I just don't know how we can maneuver through this without it affecting the music—or worse, without it costing us each other. We're barely speaking now, and we aren't even in a relationship. What happens when we are? What happens when we're fully committed and can't move past our differences?

That thought sits heavy as I pull a vintage Roberto Cavalli mixed-print dress from the back of my closet. I've been saving it for a special occasion. It's revealing in both the front and the back, and hugs my body in all the best ways.

What better occasion than to wear it to make my best

friend—who is more than just my best friend, who I'm not really speaking to, who I absolutely want to be with, and who I am actively pretending I don't want to be with—jealous?

Not one to kill my own delusions, I decide that this logic makes perfect sense to me. If I can't talk to Tyrell, I can at least remind him of exactly what he's missing.

I move to the mirror, running the diffuser through my curls. Big hair. A bold dress. Killer shoes. Makeup that complements without overpowering. If nothing else, I'll walk into that restaurant confident, composed, and unforgettable.

I grab my purse and keys and head out the door, holding onto that confidence as tightly as I can.

My homegirl Sydney is notoriously late, so I'm not expecting anything different when I pull up to her birthday dinner. The reservation says 8:00, but I get there at 8:30. Surprisingly, most of her guests have already arrived at the upscale spot in West Adams. It's my first time at this Black-owned establishment, and I take in all of the details of the interior—the rustic tables and décor, the exposed brick walls that give the space an old-fashioned, homey feel.

As I'm admiring the architecture, a familiar scent fills my nose.

I'd recognize that fragrance anywhere, because the last time she wore it, I was all over her. We barely made it to our dinner reservation. The notes of lilies, rose, musk, and sandalwood pair too well with her body's pheromones, pulling me in every time she wears it.

I smell her before I see her.

I turn my head just in time to catch Melody strutting past me in a tight dress that shows off every bit of her hourglass figure. Her hair is styled my favorite way—big loose curls that hang past her shoulders and sit high on her head. Her heels are sky-high, made even more noticeable by the slit in her dress, exposing the thickness and length of her long, brown, well-moisturized legs.

She looks damn good.

And she knows it.

And I know she wants me to know it too.

We both knew the other would be here tonight. Sydney is a part of our college friend group, and rarely do any of us get together anymore. I couldn't miss tonight, and I knew Mel wouldn't either. She's already greeted most of the people here, including her best friend Tisha, before making her way toward me.

I brace myself.

Mel is beautiful, but she's also all over the place. She doesn't know what she wants, and I'm starting to realize I don't know how much longer I can stick around waiting for her to figure it out.

"Hey," she says, opening her arms to hug me.

I breathe her in, instinctively resting my hand against the part of her dress that exposes her back.

"Hey. You look beautiful," I say, my voice low enough that no one could possibly overhear.

"Thank you," she replies, her voice matching mine. "You look handsome yourself."

"You're wearing that perfume I like."

She laughs sweetly, then says, matter-of-factly, "Actually, I'm wearing the perfume *I* like."

We loosen our hold on each other, but don't fully step away, gazing directly in each other's eyes—until we're interrupted by the birthday girl herself.

"Hey, everyone!" Sydney calls out, looking beautiful in her long, gray ruched dress.

Melody and I pull apart to greet her, and I make my way to my seat on the opposite side of the table from Mel.

I can't allow myself to show any more vulnerability towards this woman, I tell myself.

At least not here.

I'm seated next to Tisha at a table of nine, while Tyrell sits at the opposite end of the table near most of our guy friends. The rest of the party has been seated for about fifteen minutes now—ordering drinks, catching up, slipping easily into conversation. Tyrell and I, however, have been doing something else entirely: sneaking looks at each other, saying everything with our eyes that we refuse to say out loud.

Tisha pokes me while I'm pretending to look at the menu —somewhat considering what I want to eat, but mostly, tracking Tyrell from across the table.

"So...wassup with you and Ty?" she whispers. "Why y'all not sitting together, but giving each other bedroom eyes?"

I laugh louder than intended and clap a hand over my mouth, hoping I didn't just draw attention to myself.

"We are *not* giving each other bedroom eyes," I whisper. "And besides, I see him all the time. I want to sit with my friends that I don't get to see often."

"Mmhmm. Then why are y'all not talking?"

"We're in a weird space right now. Work stuff."

Tisha squints at me, lips pursed, forehead creasing in a way that tells me she doesn't believe a word I just said. The fact that she's clocking this so easily tells me Tyrell and I are not hiding things nearly as well as I thought.

"Why are you looking at me like that?" I ask, defensive already.

"Girl, you know I know there's more going on than what you're telling me."

"Give the waiter your order," I say quickly, "and then come with me to the ladies' room."

Once we're inside the large, dimly lit restroom, Tisha immediately starts questioning me.

"What's going on? Spill it."

"Well..." I start, tone apprehensive. "Ty and I—"

"Bitch!" she interrupts. "It's about time y'all started fucking!"

"Correction. We *were* fucking. Now we're not. And we're barely even talking like that, as you can see."

I start to pace, irritation and anxiety mixing as I replay the situation for the hundredth time.

"Okay, slow down," Tisha says. "Start from the beginning. How did this even happen?"

"Okay, so a couple of months ago, he called me one night just to see what I was doing. It was a Friday and I was cooking, so of course he came over. He suggested going out for drinks, so we ended up at a bar nearby. Then G texted the group chat saying he was going to Dirty on 85, so we stopped there. We were drinking and dancing and shit...just being very flirty."

Tisha nods, invested.

"I do the *On A High Note* podcast a few days later, and they ask me if I'd ever date him. I say maybe, if I thought he was serious. A few days after that, he calls me and asks if he can take me on a date—because he *is* serious."

"Oh my God, Mel! How was the date?"

"Honestly, it was great. He was the perfect gentleman. Once I got over my nerves, I was able to enjoy myself a lot more. Conversation was flowing. We damn near closed out the restaurant. He walked me upstairs when he dropped me off and…yeah."

"The rest is history," Tisha smirks. "Okay, but let's get to the important part. How was the sex?"

"*Girl.*"

A very vivid flashback crosses my mind, and I start to fan myself.

"Damnnnn, Mel. That good?"

"Better than good. Amazing. He knew exactly what to do and how to do it."

Tisha leans back, arms crossed. "So, let me get this straight…the sex is amazing, y'all obviously get along well, and the chemistry is there. I'm not understanding the issue?"

"It's me, honestly," I admit. "Ty wants a relationship, and I've been shutting it down because I think it's bad for business. If things go south between us, what happens to our careers?"

"Mel," she says gently, "you two have a bond that most people pray for. The respect, the care, the love is already there between you two. That's a rare thing, babe."

I sigh, knowing Tisha's right. "I'm just scared, Tish. I don't want to lose him. I'd rather scale it back and maintain our friendship than put that at risk. Ty's too important to me to lose him."

"You're already about to lose him if you don't get it together," she counters. "You keep pushing him away, and eventually he's going to stop coming back."

I feel myself getting emotional. "You know I'm no good at this shit. Nobody hates feelings more than me."

I grab the tissue Tisha hands me as my eyes sting.

"And then I ran into him with Natalie when I was out with

Victor Washington," I continue. "I spent the whole night pissed, even though I basically pushed him to do that. Jaime suggested dating other people to throw the media off, and I don't think either of us thought the other person would actually *do* it. Seeing him with Natalie brought out a level of jealousy I didn't even know I had, girl."

"Well, that was a shitty idea," Tisha says, bluntly. "Even worse that you both followed through with it."

She squeezes my hand. "I know everything that went down between you and your mom has you on defense, but you have to trust Ty. And you have to trust *yourself*. Don't miss out on love because you're afraid, Mel."

"It's so hard not to be afraid," I whisper. "I feel like eventually, I'm going to lose everyone I love. I just...I don't want to put myself in that position."

"Melody," she says firmly, "listen to me. *Just. Try.* Love is always a risk, but this one is worth it."

I don't even realize the tears sliding down my face as Tisha wraps me into her arms, pressing tissues into my hand.

CHAPTER 42

Tyrell

Tisha and Melody return from the bathroom after a few minutes, and something about Mel immediately feels off. I study her face more closely. Her eyes look glossy, lashes a little clumped—like she's been...crying?

When she finally looks up and catches me staring, I give her a questioning look, silently asking if she's okay. She mouths, *I'm good,* then turns away like she didn't just gut-punch me with concern.

She's not good.

And I'm not pretending I don't see it.

I have to figure out what's going on with Mel. I just need a chance to talk to her.

We all leave the restaurant soon after and head to a lounge to keep Sydney's birthday going. Everyone settles into our section, ordering drinks, laughing, falling into familiar rhythms. I try to follow along, but my attention never really leaves Melody.

When she slips away from the table—probably headed to the restroom—I don't hesitate. I follow her, knowing this might be my only opportunity.

"Mel," I call out. "Wait up."

She turns her head to me, face scrunched.

"What's up?"

"I wanna talk to you."

"Tyrell. Not here."

"You looked like you were crying earlier. You haven't been talking to me. I just wanna make sure you're good."

"I'm fine, Tyrell," she says, stiffly. "Everything is not about you."

Something in me snaps.

"Oh, because everything has to be about *you*, right?" I fire back. "Whatever Mel wants, when she wants it—and when she doesn't want it anymore, it's suddenly unimportant."

I'm exhausted. Tired of playing these games with her. Tired of chasing clarity. No matter how I may feel about Melody, I can't keep doing this back-and-forth.

Either we're going to do this, or we're not. And right now, it feels like *not*.

"You've got a lot of nerve saying all of this," she shoots back, "after you were just hugged up with the person you told me on our first date that you weren't worried about. I see you've got a selective memory."

At this point, we're standing too close, faces tight with frustration, neither of us willing to back down.

"Come on."

I grab her hand before she can protest and guide her quickly away from the restroom, maneuvering through the crowd and out the front door. I keep walking in the opposite direction of the lounge until we're far enough from the entrance that no one can overhear us.

She yanks her hand free.

"For the record, the only reason I let you drag me out here

is because I didn't want to cause a scene," she says. "What do you want, Tyrell?"

"I want to talk," I say, voice tight. "I want to figure out what the fuck is going on between us. We're not speaking. Things are past awkward. We can't keep going on like this."

I am visibly frustrated, as is she. And underneath all of it, as much as we both are fed up with one another, there's still something pulling us toward each other—proof that neither one of us truly wants to walk away.

"I don't think it's a good idea for us to pursue anything outside of a business relationship, Tyrell."

The sharpness of her words cuts through me.

"You say that," I reply, "yet, you can't keep your eyes off of me. You say that, yet you were just crying in a bathroom to your best friend not even an hour ago. I'm pretty sure those tears were about me, and I'm pretty sure it's not because you're done with me. They're because no matter how much you want to bury how you feel, you can't."

I pause, then say the part I've been holding in.

"And I damn sure can't deny how I feel about you."

"We can't always get what we want," she fires back. "That's the point. In a perfect world, we get this amazing friends-to-lovers story *and* a flourishing career. In real life though, it's way more complicated. A lot is at stake."

She exhales sharply.

"We're new artists in an R&B space that is already hard to break into and even harder to thrive in. If we're barely talking after just a few dates, what happens when we're more invested and more serious issues are at play? I don't trust us to fight and move on like it's nothing."

"You're self-sabotaging," I say. "And you're putting shit on me that I haven't even done. We've known each other since we were nineteen. There have been plenty of times we've been annoyed with one another, been fed up, needed our space—and we always found our way back."

I reach for her hands, grounding myself before saying what matters most.

"Melody, I need you to trust me. I know you're scared of this blowing up in your face. And deep down, I know it's because of everything you've lost—everything you've been through with your parents."

My voice softens.

"But don't push me away, though, because I really care about you. And I really love you."

She closes her eyes, fighting back tears as she squeezes my hands.

"I'm scared, Ty," she admits. "I don't think I can lose anyone else close to me."

I pull her into my arms when the tears finally fall, hugging her as tight as I can. I pick her head up so she can look me in my eyes.

"I'm not going anywhere," I tell her. "There's no problem that we can't work through."

I lean down and kiss her pillowy lips, slow and sure, reminding both of us of what we've been missing.

"I love you, babe," I whisper.

"I love you more," she pants.

"Then love me enough to trust me."

She tilts her head, studying me, then breaks into a small smile.

"I'll do my best."

"Let's go."

"We can't just leave our friends in the middle of a party, Ty. Let's go b-"

"I wasn't asking."

I take her hand and lead her toward my car. I expect an argument. Instead, she stays quiet—then smirks.

I smile back.

I might've smiled the whole way home.

We barely make it inside my apartment before we're kissing—messy, urgent, like we've both been holding our breath for too long. Hands everywhere, as we scramble to remove each other's clothing. I wasn't planning on taking my time. I needed Melody to feel—without question—how inevitable this is. How inevitable *we* are.

Her skin is warm and impossibly soft under my palms, like it remembers me. Like it's been waiting. The way she presses into me makes my dick throb, anticipation tightening low in my stomach as I guide us toward my bedroom, our tongues tangling, my hands memorizing the curves of her body all over again. The faint trace of basil and citrus from her cocktail still lingers on her lips, pulling me in deeper.

She breaks the kiss first, pushing me back against the wall. Her mouth trails down my neck, my chest, gradual now—intentional. The soft drag of her lips sends a shiver through me, low moans filling the room, thick with want. I fumble with my pants, desperate, but she's already there—on her knees, looking up at me like she knows exactly what she's about to do to me—

the promise of her pretty lips wrapped around my hardness sending fire through my body.

I stare down at her as her tongue slowly swirls the tip of my dick. Her hands are smooth and sure, shea-butter soft as she strokes me, and when she takes me into her mouth, I have to brace myself against the wall. She's sucking and stroking and squeezing me with the back of her throat—the proof of her commitment dripping down her chin—while she works her mouth and hands together, nearly undoing me.

"Show me how much you love me, Kitty," I grunt, fingers threading into her curls. She chokes herself on me before pulling off with a *pop*.

"Fuck, Mel." I bite my lip, damn near drawing blood when she takes me back in her mouth. My chest rises and falls as she sucks me from base to tip, like her throat was molded for my dick. Her mouth is warm, and hot, and wet, and she's staring me directly in my eyes with no care that she's about to ruin me. I feel myself on the brink of my orgasm, but hold back so that I can savor the moment.

"Yeah, baby. Take all your dick, Kitty." I manage to coach her, brushing her hair away from her face.

She moans around my dick, hollowing out her cheeks, sucking me like there's a pot of gold at the end, and my body feels close to its release.

"Fuuuucccckk, babe! I'm about to cum."

She cups my balls with one hand, the other stroking my shaft as her mouth chases her hand, and I grunt my release down her throat.

"Shit, baby," I growl, a hunger growing inside me.

I lift her chin, guiding her up to me, before plunging my tongue into her mouth. I'm desperately holding onto her waist while our tongues battle for dominance—and in this moment right here, I know I need this shit forever.

I lay us back on the bed, pulling her up to straddle my waist.

"Sit on my face."

I don't give her time to respond before I grab her thighs and pull her body up until her pussy meets my lips. She shivers when I flick my tongue across her clit, my hands resting on her thighs as I take in her scent and count my blessings. I dip my tongue in her center as she rides her new throne, groaning while I lick, suck, and savor the sweetest thing I've ever tasted.

She whines above me when I place one hand softly on her back, pressing her down to hands-and-knees, using the middle fingers of my other to massage her inner walls while I continue to lap at her essence. I still need more of her—I rotate my hand and insert a finger in her ass, gently moving it in and out while I devour the sweetest, most addictive thing I've ever tasted.

"Mmmm, you feel so good," her voice is labored and charged. "Please, don't stop."

I feel her tense up. Her fight or flight must kick in, because she tries to lift up. She tries to run. I grip her waist tighter, holding her in place while my mouth, tongue, and hands remind her *whose* she is. Her legs begin to shake, and her pussy tightens around my fingers, her balance faltering as her orgasm hits.

"Oh. My. God. Fuck, Ty!"

Her juices coat my beard, and I make sure to get every drop, even though I'm eager to get inside of her. I make quick work of pinning Melody down on her back, kissing her as I strap up. She watches me with a look so full of desire, it makes me smile as I enter her. I hit bottom with one stroke, and she exhales with pure pleasure. We stay there not moving for just a heartbeat, lost in each other's eyes. I take my time, easing in and out, not rushing, wanting to stay in this moment for as long as possible.

Her hand cups my face as she whispers, "I missed you. So. Much."

I slow stroke her deep, swirling my hips against her pelvis, groaning at the sounds she makes against my ear.

"You missed me, or you missed this dick, Kitty?"

She grips my throat, pulling my lips to hers.

"Both."

The huskiness in her voice nearly undoes me.

"Shit, Mel!"

I pick up the pace, burying myself fully inside her with each stroke. She pulls my face close and moans, "You ready for me to ride that dick?"

Before another second passes, I flip her over, pinching her nipples as she arches her back and begins to grind on top of me. My thumb moves against her clit, and she cries out in a melody I've never heard before, but will now spend my life chasing. Her body stiffens, and I meet her rhythm, driving her closer until she grips me and cries out as she cums.

I flip her onto her back again, needing to look into her eyes while I pour my love inside of her.

"I love you so much," she breathes into my mouth.

I kiss her hard, the sounds of our bodies moving together, the only soundtrack, until I can't hold back anymore.

The way Mel and I made love was unlike anything I'd ever experienced. Our eyes stayed locked, hands entwined, kisses slow and deep as time blurred around us. Now we lie tangled beneath my sheets, the room quiet except for our breathing. It's past midnight, and exhaustion finally settles in.

"You wore me out, girl."

She laughs softly, her voice rough with fatigue.

"Sleep. I know you're tired."

She pulls me to her chest, and I rest my head there, listening to her heartbeat. Her fingers drift through my locs, languid, absentminded. This feels real. Safe. Like something I should've protected better.

My eyes stay closed, but my thoughts don't rest.

There's a flicker of regret I can't ignore—not loud enough to disrupt the moment, but present all the same. A reminder of a choice I made when I was running from what was right in front of me. Something careless. Something I wish I could undo.

I hold her a little tighter, as if that might anchor us both in this version of now—the one where nothing else exists but us.

"Ty?"

"Yeah, babe?"

"I love you."

The words land heavier than anything else tonight. I press my lips to her hair, breathing her in.

"I love you more," I whisper.

And as sleep finally claims me, I hold onto the hope that this—us—can stay untouched.

I text my girls in the group chat, already knowing they're pissed about me leaving the club with Tyrell and not saying a word.

Ummmm…hey girls! About last night…

KIM

You finally pulled Tyrell's dick out of your mouth long enough to send us a text?

SYDNEY

Bitch, you could've told us you were leaving!

Shut up, Kim! I'm sorry, y'all. Tyrell and I were having a conversation and got caught up in the moment. I wanted to come back and join y'all, but he…had other plans.

TISHA

I'm not mad at you, sis. I would've done the same. Fuck y'all! I'm leaving with my man.

KIM

So, does this mean that you two are finally
done being in denial about being in love?

We were never in denial, Kim. We just
needed some time.

SYDNEY

Fifteen years, Mel?!

TISHA

It doesn't matter, Syd! They finally got it
together.

KIM

Okay, sooooo…can we get the details,
Mel? You know there used to be so many
rumors on our campus that Tyrell was
packing.

SYD

Yeah, that bitch Brittany would not shut up
about how big his dick was.

Chile, she wasn't lying.

TISHA

Oh, shit!

SYD

KIM

I know that's right, honey. I see why you left
the club and let him knock the Sonic coins
out of you.

SYD

Ty's a little on the lighter side, Mel. Is it
pink???

KIM

SYD!!!

NO, SYDNEY. Omg

SYD

Damn, I was just asking. We all have our
preferences.

TISHA

I would rather not have the image of Tyrell's
dick being pink in my head.

KIM

I'm just glad our girl is getting some dick
now. Bitch ain't get laid since Obama was
still in office.

Don't do me like that!

Y'all are so ridiculous. I'll hit you up when I
get home.

KIM

Awwww, shit!

TISHA

Enjoy round two...or whichever round this
is.

I toss my phone onto the bed beside me, stifling my laughter so I don't wake Tyrell. My girls are wild, but they're right—it *is* about time.

I glance over at him, his arm heavy around my waist, his breathing slow and even. I'm hoping this is it for us. That we can finally move forward without fear running the show.

He asked me to trust him.

And for the first time in a long time, I think I'm ready to.

That morning, after I drop Melody at her apartment and answer the whirlwind of texts and calls from our friends asking where the hell we disappeared to last night, I finally make it home. All I want to do is relax, catch the Lakers game, and let my mind settle.

As I flip through channels, my phone lights up with an incoming call.

Natalie.

I freeze for a moment, staring at her name on the screen. We haven't spoken in weeks, so I'm not sure why she'd be calling me now. Still, I welcome it. I've needed to end whatever this was between us for a while, and this feels like the moment. Overdue, uncomfortable, but necessary. I don't want bad blood—especially not with someone I once cared about.

I take a deep breath and answer.

"Hey, Nat. How are you?"

"Hey, Ty. We need to talk. You busy?"

Her voice is cool, clipped. Not angry, but not warm either. My first thought is that she's calling to end things, too, and I almost feel relieved. Maybe this will be easier than I've been building it up to be.

"No, I've got time," I say. "Everything good?"

There's a pause. Just long enough for my stomach to tighten.

"Tyrell," she says, her voice steady but weighted, "I'm pregnant."

Pregnant?

The word hangs in the air, heavy and unreal. I don't respond right away because my brain refuses to catch up to what my ears just heard. A baby. With Natalie. Just minutes ago, I was replaying the night with Melody in my head, still riding the high of finally being honest with each other. Now, everything feels like it's tilting.

A baby changes everything.

How was this even possible? is my first thought, followed immediately by everything else—Mel, my family, my career, the optics, the responsibility. I never wanted to bring a child into the world with someone I wasn't in love with. I never wanted to be a halfway father, or a man who got it wrong from the start.

"Ty?" Natalie's voice cuts through the silence. She sounds anxious. "You there?"

"Yeah," I say finally. "I'm here. I'm just...really surprised. Trying to figure out how this happened."

Natalie lets out a soft chuckle. "I think you know how this happened."

"I thought we used protection."

"We did. I think it ripped without either of us realizing."

My stomach twists as my mind instantly goes back to that night. After Natalie and I ran into Melody and Victor at Nobu, I was infuriated. Seeing them close and kissing one another made me jealous beyond comprehension, and all logic went out of the window. My petty revenge fuck did nothing but give me a baby I'm not ready for, and two women that will forever be impacted by my recklessness.

"How are you feeling about all of this?" I ask Natalie, trying to remove my personal feelings from it. Regardless of our relationship status, I do want to be supportive. I can't even imagine how she's processing all of this.

"Scared. Shocked. Disappointed. Confused. So many things. I don't know how to feel or what to do, especially when we aren't even together."

"You know I care about you, Nat. We'll figure it out together. You don't have to deal with this alone." I hope the sincerity of my words translates through the phone.

"I know. And thank you for saying that. But...there's something else, Ty."

I don't think I can handle another bomb being dropped on me right now.

"What's up?"

"Remember I told you that I was waitlisted for Columbia Law School? Well, I got in. I'm moving to New York this summer."

"What?!" I pause, then recover. "I mean—congratulations. You know I'm happy for you. But where does this leave me and the baby?"

Don't get me wrong, I don't want to be with Natalie. But if I'm going to be a father, I'm going to make sure I'm an active one. I'll be damned if I only see my kid on holidays and special occasions. I can't be the father this child deserves if we live on opposite sides of the country.

"Ty," Natalie pauses, her voice softening. "I'm not keeping this baby."

Damn. My heart sinks a little. I've always wanted to be a father. And yeah, this situation is far from ideal, but I'm more than willing to figure it out.

"I mean...your body, your choice, of course. I would still like to have a little bit of say in this. Don't you think that's a decision we make together?"

"Be realistic, Tyrell. I can't put my future on hold for a baby I'm not even ready for—and for a man who's in love with someone else."

How does she know?

"Nat, I-"

"Don't, Tyrell. I know you don't want to be with me, and you've made that abundantly clear. I saw the way you were watching Melody and Victor at Nobu. I've heard the interviews and the rumors. You love her. That's the real reason why you don't want anything to do with me."

I don't know what to say. "I'm sorry, Natalie. My intention was never to hurt you. I fucked up." I needed to be honest—with her and with myself.

"Ty-"

"Let me finish. You're right about Melody and me. I do have feelings for her. We haven't quite figured things out yet, and I shouldn't have dragged you into our mess. I apologize for that. Our relationship shifted recently, and we've just been trying to figure shit out. I want you to know that Mel and I were very much just friends while you and I were rocking heavy. Don't think that I was just fucking both of y'all at the same time—that wasn't the case. After Valentine's Day with you, I realized that something was missing. I didn't feel the chemistry.”

“You mean the chemistry you have with Melody?”

No sense in lying now.

“Yeah,” I say, ashamed. “I should’ve been a man and told you how I felt. I didn’t want to hurt you.”

“So, you thought stringing me along was better?”

“It wasn’t. I know that. And I’m not proud of how I treated you. You were great to me. You’re an amazing woman. It’s just…you’re not the one for me.”

There it is. I’ve put it all out there. A part of me feels relieved, but a bigger part feels like absolute shit. I never meant for things to get this far.

“I’m really sorry, Natalie.”

“I know. And I know you didn’t mean for things to get this far. But they did, and now I have to deal with the consequences. There’s no way I can do law school and build the career I want with a baby on the way. I know you’d be an amazing father. This just isn’t the right time for me to think about kids. I hope you can respect that.”

“I do. I’m not here to pressure you. I understand the position you’re in, and I support whatever you decide.”

“Thank you, Ty. I know this is a lot. But neither of us is in the space for a baby right now. You have to think about your career and future just as much as I do.”

“You’re right. This is bad timing all around. I respect your decision, Nat.”

“I plan to take care of this next week.”

Damn. She had the appointment booked before she even told me she was pregnant.

“Just out of curiosity…were you ever going to tell me?”

“Honestly? No. I was just going to handle it and move on with my life.”

“Wow. Okay. Well…I’m glad you told me.”

"I'm glad I did, too. I would've felt guilty keeping this from you. My friend Joy said she saw you and Melody walking out of the club hand in hand. After that, I was furious and almost didn't tell you at all. She convinced me I needed to."

Shit. I thought we were being *discreet* last night.

"Can I come with you to the clinic? I don't want you to do this alone."

"No," she says quickly. "You can't risk being seen with me. Joy's coming. I'll hit you up after."

She's completely shutting me out. I can't say I blame her, but it doesn't feel good knowing I wasn't even a consideration. She wasn't even going to tell me at all.

"Can I at least drive you there and back?"

"That won't be necessary. But thank you."

"Uhh-okay. I'm sorry again, Natalie."

"We both laid down and made choices, Ty. It's easy to blame you, but I have to take responsibility too. I saw the inconsistency and stayed, hoping things would change. I have no one to blame but myself."

Her words cut deep. I don't want to be the kind of man who hurts women through indecision. That shit is not okay.

"No. This isn't on you. And I'm going to be there for you however I can. Call me if you need anything."

"I will," she says softly. "And Ty...thank you for understanding. I know this is hard for you, too."

"It is. But we'll get through it."

"We will."

We hang up, and I take a long breath. I've put myself in a fucked up situation. I hurt a woman who didn't deserve it. And Melody—I can't keep this from her. If I want a future with her, she deserves the truth. I'm not starting a relationship on lies.

I have to talk to her.

My phone rings on a Wednesday afternoon while I'm in bed, taking an actual day off. I called Ty earlier this morning to see if he wanted to go to breakfast and talk, but his phone went straight to voicemail. I've been trying to act unbothered by the change in our dynamic, but it's a strange adjustment. To go from friends to lovers, to just co-workers, and then back to lovers in such a short amount of time has been a complete rollercoaster.

I see his name come across my phone screen and immediately pick up. I hope we can finally talk and figure things out.

"Hey."

"Hey, you."

"I called you earlier today. Your phone went straight to voicemail."

"Yeah, I turned my phone off. I just needed some time to think without any distractions."

There's tension in Ty's voice, and it immediately makes me worry.

"Is everything okay?"

"Yeah. I have to talk to you about something, Mel."

"Um…okay. I don't like the way your voice sounds, so it can't be good."

I hear him exhale on the other end of the phone.

"So…Natalie called me a few days ago and told me she was pregnant. She decided not to keep it, and today is the day she took care of that. I-"

My heart sinks. "I'm sorry…say that again."

"Mel, please. Nat-"

"I know you didn't just tell me that you got somebody else pregnant." My hands start shaking. I jump out of bed and begin pacing my apartment, trying to calm myself down.

"You know I didn't mean for this to happen, Mel."

"So, your dick just slipped and fell inside of her?"

"I'm not making any excuses. I know I shouldn't have had sex with Natalie. It was a mistake, and it will never happen again."

"Why should I believe that? How can you tell me you're in love with me one minute and have raw sex with another woman the next? That's not love, Tyrell."

"I do love you, Melody. I care about you. I want us to work. I made a bad decision that I really regret."

"You and I never even had sex raw. I can't believe you gave your body to somebody like that. You got so mad at me for being out with Victor, and you were fucking Natalie the whole time!"

My voice keeps escalating, and it's taking everything in me not to explode.

"We used protection, but things happen. I wanted to tell you the truth. I'm not proud of how I moved, and it was childish. I really wanna work past this, Mel. I don't want there to be any lies between us.

"It was extremely childish of you. I can't believe you would hurt me like this."

"I know, and I apologize. I would never want to hurt you. You know how much you mean to me."

"Do I? So, tell me—next time you get mad at me, are you going to go fuck the first thing walking?"

"Melody, stop. You know I'm not like that." His voice rises to match my intensity.

"And you have the nerve to be offended? I'm not out here moving like you!"

"You're not innocent, Mel. I saw you kissing up on Victor at Nobu. Holding his hand and shit. Making faces at me because you knew it would make me lose it. You were playing a game just like I was. I'm just the one who lost."

Now, I'm furious.

"I didn't fuck him, Tyrell."

"What?"

"I didn't sleep with Victor. Seeing you out with Natalie made me realize how much I missed you. How much I cared about you. I couldn't stand seeing you with someone else. I told myself right then and there that I needed to stop playing and admit I'm in love with you."

"You are?"

"Yes, Tyrell. I am. I called you this morning to see if we could sit down and talk. Work things out."

"Baby, I-"

"Don't call me that. You got somebody else pregnant. You didn't give a fuck about me when you were laid up with Natalie and made a baby."

"Mel, Natalie's moving to New York this summer for law school. Nothing is tying us together. She didn't keep the baby."

"I don't give a damn if she did like Issa Rae and tossed that baby away. The point is, you made a baby with her. You trusted her with your body and didn't think twice about how it would affect me."

"You're right. And I'm going to keep apologizing to you until you forgive me—and even after that. I don't want to be with her. I never wanted to be with her. I love you, Melody."

"You have a really interesting way of showing that."

"Please, can I come over and talk to you? Give me a chance to make this right."

"I need time, Tyrell. I'm really upset. I feel like you played me."

"Baby, I would never play you. Please, let's just talk. I love y-"

"I'm done talking about this. Don't call me."

I hang up and throw my phone onto the couch before dropping down beside it. When he calls back, I send his ass right to voicemail.

I feel everything at once—anger, frustration, disappointment. I expected more from Tyrell. I should've never gotten involved with him to begin with.

How can I be in love with someone who almost had a child with someone else?

April 2012
Sophomore Year

"Ty, why the hell do you have me here on a Wednesday at 1 am? You know I have class in the morning!"

"I know, I know. And I'm sorry," he says quickly. "But I didn't want to hold off until tomorrow. My mind was working in overdrive. I needed you to hear this."

I yawn, instantly regretting the fact that I glanced over at my phone thirty minutes ago and actually picked up when I saw Tyrell's name. Silly me for thinking I was being a good friend. Apparently, Ty had an idea for a song that just *couldn't wait*, and that meant I needed to be at his dorm ASAP.

I plop down on the couch as he sits at the bench of his piano.

"I don't know how useful I'll be at this time of the night," I say, rubbing my eyes, "but I'll do my best since you woke me out of my sleep for this."

"It'll be worth it," he replies.

His deep voice fills the room as his fingers move across the keys, playing the softest melody. He hums along, sultry and inviting, the sound immediately pulling me in. Whatever annoyance I walked in with starts to fade.

"This is good, Ty," I admit. "I like it. Reminds me of D'Angelo a little."

"I thought you might like it," he says with a grin, pulling out a notebook and tossing it my way, along with a pen.

An hour passes without either of us noticing. We're deep into writing a song about a couple tired of arguing, wanting to remember why they fell in love in the first place—how much they need each other, emotionally and physically.

When we finally pause, Tyrell leans over and pulls me into a hug, clearly excited about what we just created. When he lets go, I don't move right away. I lean into his shoulder, comfortable in a way that feels dangerous if I think about it too long.

"Did you write this song for Brittany?" I ask.

Tyrell laughs and looks down at me.

"Hell, no."

"Damn," I say. "You didn't have to say it like that."

"I didn't." Tyrell sits up, turning his body toward me. "But the way you asked makes me feel like you *don't* want it to be about her." A smirk tugs at his lips, but his eyes are searching. "You don't like her, do you?"

"I was just asking," I reply quickly, rolling my eyes. "You're in a relationship and just wrote a song about arguing with your girl and making up. Silly me for assuming it was about your girlfriend."

I'm trying to sound casual, but the truth is, I really do want to know what's going on between him and Brittany. Because the thought of having a crush on this man—and helping him write a love song about his girlfriend—makes my stomach twist.

"Nah," he chuckles. "It's not about her. And you didn't answer my question."

"What question?" I ask, even though I know exactly what he means.

His expression turns serious. "Do you like Brittany for me?"

"No," I answer immediately.

The word just flies out of my mouth, and I rush to backtrack.

"I mean—she's cool. She's ju-"

"She's just not *you*, right?"

My breath catches.

"What do you mean by that, Tyrell?"

We are staring at each other now, the air between us suddenly heavy. This doesn't feel like a conversation two friends should be having. It feels like something else entirely.

"I mean," he moves closer to me, "you don't like her for me because you think it should be you."

"Tyrell, you're cr-"

He presses his index finger to my lips, and everything inside me lights up. I close my eyes without thinking, my body reacting before my mind can catch up.

"You don't have to respond, Mel," he murmurs. "I already know what it is. When you're ready to stop playing games, I'll be here."

He pulls his hand away, smiles like he didn't just completely knock the air out of my chest, and turns back to his keyboard. His fingers find the melody again as he hums the lyrics we wrote, completely at ease.

I force myself to act unbothered. I grab the notebook and pretend to read over the lyrics.

I don't tell Tyrell that he's absolutely right.

CHAPTER 49

Melody

I'm still trying to process the bomb Tyrell dropped on me earlier today. How could he get another woman pregnant? Things happen, yes—but we had slept together just weeks before that night at Nobu, and then again after. I don't understand how he could claim to be in love with me, say he wants to be with me, yet be so careless.

What if Natalie hadn't been so focused on her career and decided to keep her baby? We wouldn't have had a future then. There's no way I could've been a part of that child's life—attending milestone events, showing support—while knowing my true feelings for Ty. All of this is giving me a headache.

I need to talk to someone. Immediately.

My uncle Keith has been my safe space since I was a little girl. Whenever I've needed a logical perspective, tough love, words of encouragement, or a good hug, he's always there. I don't trust myself not to do something stupid right now, so I dial his number.

"Hey, Uncle."

"Hey, Babygirl. You okay?"

The exhaustion in my voice must be a dead giveaway. "What do *you* know?"

He laughs. "I don't know anything yet. But I hear it in your voice. What's wrong?"

"Can I come over and talk to you? I'll bring dinner."

"You never have to ask."

An hour later, I'm parked in my uncle's driveway and unlocking his door.

"Melody?" his deep voice echoes out.

"I'm here. Can you help me with the bags?"

Uncle Keith walks out of his office, fully dressed in jeans and an embroidered navy button-down. I lean in to hug him, and he kisses my forehead.

"You look nice," I say. "What were you doing all day?"

"Minding my black ass business," he replies, glancing down at the grocery bags. "I thought you said you were bringing dinner?"

"I did. Dinner for *you* to make."

I kiss him on the cheek and run into the kitchen before he can kick me out.

"I should've known your trifling ass would swindle me into labor," he mutters, lightly tapping my head as he passes me in the kitchen.

As we unpack groceries behind his large kitchen island, he finally asks, "So, what's got you this upset?"

"It's Tyrell."

Keith rolls his eyes. "I'm going to start charging y'all by the minute for my advice."

"He called you, too?!"

The fact that Keith and Tyrell have been talking about what's been going on between us shouldn't surprise me. Keith is one of the few positive male figures in Ty's life, and he depends on Keith a lot for advice and wisdom. Normally, I don't mind sharing my uncle and find their relationship to be endearing, but today, it does nothing but irk me.

"He came by a couple of weeks ago to talk to me about a few things. And no, I'm not telling you what we talked about."

"What? You're *my* uncle."

"And I don't tell people's business. You know that."

I roll my eyes. "Whatever. He called me today. Do you know this fool went and got Natalie pregnant?"

Keith's eyes go wide. "Oh, shit! I didn't see that one coming."

"Neither did I. She already went to the clinic. Apparently, she's moving to New York for law school and didn't want to keep the baby."

Keith ponders this for a moment. If he is upset, he doesn't let it show. "Wow. That's some wild shit. What did Ty say?"

"A bunch of bullshit. How he was sorry and he never meant for this to happen. He loves me, and he wants us to be together and blah, blah, blah. All types of shit that I wasn't in the mood to hear."

Keith chuckles, "I'm surprised your crazy ass isn't at his house cussing him out, or worse."

"Oh, I definitely thought about it. But if I see him right now, I might actually kill him. This is the safest place for everyone involved."

"Yeah, this situation is fucked up. Disappointing because he knows better. You can't want to move forward with one person and fuck the next person."

"That's exactly what I said," I reply, chopping vegetables for the fish. I convinced my uncle to make us red snapper steamed in a coconut curry sauce. I know he only agreed to cook to cheer me up, and I'll never turn down a sympathy meal.

"I'm just trying to figure out how he and Natalie even got

back talking in the first place," Keith says, genuinely confused. "That came out of nowhere."

"Actually, I'm pretty sure they slept together after the night Ty and Natalie ran into Victor and me at Nobu. You should've seen the look on his face after he saw Victor kiss me."

"Melody, are you serious?" My uncle stops cleaning the fish to stare at me, his tone turning stern.

"So...Jaime suggested we be seen with other people to take the heat off of Tyrell and me. I agreed to go on a few dates with Victor Washington, and of course, we ended up running into Natalie and Ty at one of them. He stared at our table the whole night, so yeah—I played it up. Flirted extra hard to get under his skin. It obviously worked a little too well," I sigh.

"You two are both idiots, you know that?" Keith mutters, shaking his head as he goes back to the fish.

"Okay, so it probably wasn't the best decision."

"Hell no, it wasn't! So, let me get this straight, Mel. You love Ty, he loves you, and instead of figuring the shit out, you both decide to date other people. You catch each other out with someone, and now you're mad that the consequences showed up. And let me remind you, though—both of you fucked up. Ty is just the only one that got caught."

His words hit me like a ton of bricks. I don't like it, but there's validity in his statement that I'd be foolish to argue against.

"Ouch. You didn't have to hit me with it like that. Plus, I didn't sleep with Victor."

"That's neither here nor there. You still spent time with someone else, knowing you have feelings for Ty. It's not fair to drag other people into your confusion. You can't play with people's feelings like that, Mel."

"Well, Jaime seemed to think it was a good idea," I say dryly.

"Jaime doesn't know how deep this goes, does she?"

I sigh, setting the vegetables aside and heading to the cabinet for rice. "You're right. I didn't get into details. I just explained to her that Ty and I had gone out on a couple of dates, and I wanted to take the heat off the speculation. I never told her how much we actually like each other."

"Correction," Keith says, smirking. "You didn't tell her how much y'all *love* each other."

I roll my eyes, fighting a smile. "I don't know what you're talking about."

"Mel, cut the bullshit for once. You wouldn't be over here damn near in tears if this was just a simple crush."

I groan. "You know, I really came here for a shoulder to cry on—not to be held accountable. You've completely ruined my plan, Uncle."

I shove him lightly with my shoulder, and he pulls me into a side embrace.

"The truth has to hurt sometimes, Babygirl. That's how we grow."

"I know," I exhale. "I just don't know where to go from here. I want to be angry. I want to give up. I want to pretend none of this ever happened and that Ty and I can go back to being friends and business partners—but my heart is telling me otherwise."

"Love ain't logical," Keith says gently. "Go with your heart."

I cover my hands with my face. "I don't even know where to start."

"You can start by communicating. Call him. Have an honest, open conversation. Now's not the time to be stubborn or play hardball, Mel. Lay it all out on the table."

I squeeze him a little tighter before breaking away to start on the rice. "I hate when you give me great advice. I always end up having to actually follow it."

"Please do," he laughs. "So, you can get your man back, and both of y'all can leave me the fuck alone."

We burst out laughing and go back to cooking.

Later that evening, still full from the amazing meal and wine at Uncle Keith's house, I decide to do something that I haven't made time for in a while: Go Live on TikTok.

Engaging with my supporters always lifts my mood. They crack jokes, make wild requests, and remind me why I love what I do.

I start the Live, and within seconds, people begin pouring in.

"Wassup, everyone! I just came to say hi. It's been a while!"

Hearts flood the screen. People are waving, asking about my plans for the evening, and—right on cue—asking for Ty.

User40340350396158: Where's Ty's fine ass????
MzBella67123294: Mel, can you please sing for us?
C0k0Savag3$99: We see that piano back there! Sing us a few songs, and we'll leave you alone ☺

"I'm at my Uncle's house, y'all. Ty's not here!" I laugh at all of the disappointed women in the comments.

DenimBrat342$: I don't think Ty's around y'all. Mel, show us your sexy ass uncle!

"Y'all funny! Let me ask my uncle if he'll play a few songs for you guys. Y'all know he's grumpy."

Uncle Keith appears from upstairs, changed into more relaxing clothes for the evening.

"Uncle Keith," I say, turning the phone toward him, "I'm on Live, and everyone is asking for you. They want you to play the piano."

"You don't ever know when to take your ass home, I see."

"Y'all see how bad he treats me?" I laugh at my Uncle.

Despite all his complaining, he takes a seat at the piano anyway. I prop my phone onto the small magnetic stand I carry everywhere.

"I'm in the mood for some 90s throwbacks," I tell the now 500-plus people watching. "Send me your requests."

The comments start flying—Beyonce, Lauryn Hill, Toni Braxton, Jill Scott, Chanté Moore. Then one username in particular sticks out, and I recognize Ty's burner.

TKeys12345678: Sing one for me.

I don't say anything, but I notice.

As Uncle Keith begins to play, I recognize the intro immediately—Chanté Moore's *"It's Alright."*

"I'll do a little Chanté Moore for y'all," I say softly. "Ready?"

Uncle Keith plays the beautiful melody. As the piano intro ends, I break into song.

When I'm finished, I read the outpouring of hearts and compliments.

"Thank you, guys," I smile. "I'm glad you liked that."

MrsThickAsGrits$321: Girl, you sang that song like you were singing to somebody!

MzBella67123294: It was definitely dedicated to someone. Our girl sounds like she's in love, y'all.

User596038485439592: I wonder who it is!

I laugh, shaking my head. "Y'all are so messy."

I pause, then add, more honestly than I planned, "But since you brought it up...I do want to dedicate that song to someone. I don't know what to say, except...this song is for you."

TKeys12345678: 🤍 🤍 🤍

I stay on Live for a while longer, singing along with my Uncle, enjoying the company of my supporters that always keep me grounded and remind me of why I continue to pursue my dreams.

In the back of my mind, though, I'm thinking of Tyrell.

Despite everything, I do really love him.

And I think I finally know what I need to do.

CHAPTER 50

Melody

Turns out that I didn't, in fact, know what to do.

Once the wine from that night at my Uncle's house wore off and I had a few days to sit with my thoughts, I felt lower than I had in a long time.

It's Sunday afternoon, and I'm in a shitty mood because the man I'm in love with got another woman pregnant. Even after the productive conversation with Uncle Keith, I still don't know how to process that reality. I love Tyrell—yes—but love doesn't erase betrayal, regret, hurt, or the flood of emotions I don't have the energy to name. I don't feel like going to the gym. I don't feel like writing. I don't want to be around anyone or even talk on the phone. It's just one of those days where existing feels like too much effort.

For the last hour, my only solace has been lying on the couch, doom-scrolling TikTok for recipes starring the best of Trader Joe's frozen food section.

I throw on a matching sweatshirt, lounge pants, and sneakers, then nearly sprint to my car in search of Thai chili shrimp dumplings so I can recreate the recipe I just watched.

As I'm standing in the frozen food aisle, reading the nutritional facts on a box of potstickers I definitely don't need, I hear a soft voice say my name.

"Melody?"

I assume it's a fan—or someone who recognizes me from *Anderson West*—so I put on my best smile before looking up.

My smile drops immediately.

Natalie.

She's dressed casually in leisurewear and a Dodgers cap. A very attractive man stands beside her, pushing what looks like their shared shopping cart. I don't catch what he says to her, but I hear her respond softly.

"Let me talk to her for a minute, babe. I'll meet you by the pasta."

Babe?!

And I thought I moved on fast.

She pauses, adjusts her jacket, and walks toward me.

"Natalie. Hi."

I try—and fail—to smooth the apprehension off my face, because her next words come gently, but deliberately.

"Hi, Melody. I'm sure I'm the last person you want to see right now, but I really need to talk to you...if that's okay."

The hesitation in her tone tells me that what she wants to talk to me about is serious, and I say a quick prayer in my head.

Lord, please don't let this be a 'Hello Barbara, this is Shirley' moment. And if it is, please give me the strength not to beat this bitch's ass in the middle of Trader Joe's.

"Yeah," I say, firmer than I mean to. "What's going on?"

"Well... I'm sure Tyrell told you about our...situation."

"He did. He also told me you got into law school and are moving to New York."

Let's hope that's still a thing.

"Yeah. I'm leaving in about six weeks. But that's not really what I wanted to tell you." She hesitates. "I...look, I don't know how I can say this without sounding horrible, but-"

"Please don't beat around the bush," I interrupt. "Whatever you have to say, just say it."

"It wasn't Tyrell's baby."

My face scrunches up as my brain scrambles to process what I just heard.

"What do you mean it wasn't Tyrell's baby?"

"Listen...I saw you two in the blogs. I saw the way you looked at each other at Nobu. And I could tell that night that something was off with him. I just...I was furious, Melody."

"So, your very grown ass got mad and decided to be childish and lie to a man about a pregnancy?" My voice spikes before I can stop it. "This isn't an episode of *Maury*, Natalie! What the fuck?!"

A few shoppers glance over. Not wanting to cause a scene, I lower my voice, but not the intensity.

"That was a fucked up thing to do, Natalie. I don't understand why you thought that was okay."

"I'm not saying it was," she says quickly. "But imagine being into someone who keeps dodging commitment. Someone who swears that his very beautiful, very talented best friend is really *just* his best friend. And then you see them together—hugged up, hinting at a future in interviews. You would be pissed off, too, Melody."

The hurt and anger echoes through Natalie's voice.

And annoyingly...I get it.

I sigh, knowing Natalie has every right to be upset. If I were in her shoes, I'd probably be seeing red too.

"Natalie, I'm a woman first," I say, steady but honest. "Of course, I understand how that would make any woman feel. I'm not saying Tyrell is innocent—because we both know he's far from that. But lying about being pregnant by him? I just don't understand that. There were so many other ways you could've gone about getting back at him."

I mean, was she not listening when Beyoncé said, "Best revenge is your paper?"

Natalie is quiet for a moment, eyes glassy but determined not to let the tears fall.

"I know it was stupid," she admits. "I was just...so hurt. Embarrassed. I felt like a complete idiot."

"And I get that," I say, my tone softer now. "I really do." I hesitate before adding, "It sounds like you were...in love with him."

The way her eyes brighten—just slightly, painfully—tells me everything.

"I did love him, Melody. I thought he just needed more time. I tried to give him his space. I figured with his schedule, his career...a relationship just wasn't his priority yet."

"Well," I say carefully, "you seem to have gotten over that quickly."

She lets out a small, humorless chuckle. "I know the optics look crazy, but I'll be honest with you. I started dating again after I saw your podcast interview."

My confusion is brief. It clicks almost immediately. "*On a High Note,* right?"

She nods. "It was the first time I ever heard you say 'maybe' when someone asked you about Tyrell. I knew right then that I was in trouble. That it was probably time for me to move on."

"So why not do just that?" I ask. "How do you go from being that in love to getting pregnant by another man?"

I feel like a damn detective trying to get all the information I can out of this woman, but I don't care. I need some answers.

"My ex—the guy I'm here with—called me and said he was in town for work. We went to dinner, had a few drinks, and... yeah," she shrugs. "You see how that ended."

"Does he know you told Tyrell the baby was his?"

"No," she says quickly. "He knows I was pregnant. He supported my decision because he isn't ready for a baby either. He lives in New York, so he's helping me get settled. We're working on things."

We both exhale, almost in unison. Even through the tension, I can tell a huge weight has been lifted off of her. I know first-hand what it's like to carry something heavy alone for too long.

I do have another question that I need to ask, even though it's the last thing I'd really want to know.

"Natalie, I don't mean to sound insensitive, but how sure are you that it wasn't Tyrell's baby?"

"Very," she says without hesitation. "Tyrell is *always* careful. We used protection every time. Plus, the timing just doesn't add up." She pauses, then adds quietly, "I'm surprised he never even questioned it."

"He trusted you," I say. "Probably thought you'd be the last person to lie to him about something like that."

Natalie drops her head for a moment, then nods. "You're right. He did trust me. And I feel horrible about what I did. It's completely against my character."

I believe her. I can see it in her eyes.

I could keep questioning her. I could sit in judgment a little longer. But I don't want to. The best thing for all of us to do is just...move on.

"I know you're going to tell Tyrell," she says quietly. "And I'm going to tell him the truth too...if he even gives me the chance."

The realization that I'm going to be the one to break the news to Tyrell makes me pause. It almost feels like I'd be doing Natalie a favor—but more than that, I'd rather it come from me.

"Just curious, if you didn't run into me today, would you have told Tyrell at all?"

She fidgets with her hands, then looks directly at me. "Eventually."

I nod. I don't love the answer, but I understand it.

"Well," she says, glancing toward the pasta aisle, "I should probably get back to—"

"Yeah, you do that," I cut in gently. "Take care of yourself, Natalie."

I turn to leave, but she touches my arm.

"I know this might sound strange coming from me," she says, voice sincere, "but I hope you don't let this ruin what you two have. Tyrell really loves you. And it's obvious you love him too."

I hold her gaze for a moment, then nod. "I'll remember that."

We part ways.

And as I walk down the aisle alone, one thing becomes clear—not what I'm *supposed* to do, not what anyone else thinks I should do—but what I can no longer avoid facing.

CHAPTER 51

Melody

Between the conversation I had with Uncle Keith last week and the bomb Natalie dropped on me yesterday, I'm emotionally drained. My feelings are all over the place. I'm caught between being furious with Tyrell for sleeping with Natalie, and wanting to shake Natalie for lying to him in the first place. No matter how hurt she was, lying about the paternity of a pregnancy was cruel and unnecessary.

Part of me wants to keep my conversation with Natalie to myself, just to avoid seeing the devastation on Tyrell's face when I tell him the truth. The other part of me knows I can't do that. I don't want him carrying the weight of a child that was never even his—grieving, feeling guilty, wondering about a future that doesn't even exist...

I decide to call him.

The phone rings twice before his voice comes through, raspy and low. "Hey."

"Hey. You busy? We need to talk." I keep my tone flat, careful not to give anything away.

"Never too busy for you, Mel. You wanna come by, or you want me to come to your place?"

"Come over here," I say. "I know you don't have any food in your house, and I'm too hungry to look at an empty fridge."

He scoffs softly. "I'm on my way."

Forty minutes later, my phone alerts me that I have a guest. The familiar rhythmic knock—that one I've grown embarrassingly fond of—echoes through my apartment. When I open the door, Tyrell stands there freshly shaved, locs neatly retwisted, dressed casually, but effortlessly put together.

It's annoying how much more attractive he is when I'm mad at him.

"Hey," I say quietly.

"Hey, you. Can I hug you, or are you planning to stab me?"

"Ha! A hug is fine."

He pulls me into him, one hand settling at my waist, the other resting against my back.

"What about a kiss?" he whispers in my ear.

"Now, you're pushing it," I reply, rolling my eyes.

Tyrell makes his way to my living room, detouring through the kitchen to grab a bottle of water. He sits on the couch, cautious as he takes a seat directly across from me, as if bracing for whatever's coming.

"My thoughts are all over the place," I admit. "I don't know where to start." Before I can say more, he leans forward.

"Let me say something first." He clears his throat. "I just want to apologize for putting you through all of this. It was incredibly irresponsible of me to go out with Natalie and be intimate with her. It wasn't fair to you or her, and I know I fucked up. Neither one of you deserved to be put in this position, and I truly am sorry, Mel."

"Ty, I—"

"Wait." His voice firms. "Let me finish."

He takes a deep breath. "I am in love with you, Melody. I

don't want to be with anyone but you. I really hope we can move past this—but if you can't, I understand. I'll wait. As long as it takes for you to forgive me."

The sincerity in his eyes steals the air from my lungs. And it confirms what I already know; I can't hold this in. "I appreciate that," I say carefully. "But there's something you need to know. I ran into Natalie at Trader Joe's yesterday. She pulled me to the side, and we talked."

His expression shifts—guarded now. "Okay…"

I sigh before continuing. "The baby wasn't yours, Ty. She told me. She said she only lied because she was pissed about us. She said that she was going to tell you the truth, eventually."

I watch Ty's expression go from uncertainty to surprise—and then, rage.

"What the fuck?!" His voice jumps in volume. "What do you mean the baby wasn't mine? Why the fuck would she lie about something like that?! This isn't high school. That's not something to play around with."

He jumps to his feet, pacing, arms crossed tight against his chest.

"I need to call her," he says. "I'm sorry, Mel. I know we have our own shit to work out, but I'm furious right now, and I need some answers."

I stand and step directly into his path, placing my hands on his shoulders to stop him.

"Ty. I get why you're upset. I really do. But calling her right now isn't going to help. You're angry—and rightfully so—but this needs to end clean, not in a screaming match."

He exhales sharply, eyes squeezed shut as he tries to steady himself. I cup his face, my palms warm against his beard.

"I'm not saying don't address it," I say gently. "I'm just asking you to do it when you're level-headed. Okay?"

Again, he closes his eyes and exhales, opening them to look down at me.

"Okay. Okay," he says quietly. "I'll call her in a few days."

"Thank you," I take his hand and guide him back to the couch.

"There's something else," I say. His expression is closed now, unreadable. He gestures for me to continue.

"I know I've been all over the place when it comes to us. The truth is, I spent so many years pretending I didn't have feelings for you—pushing them down because I was scared of what might happen if I didn't. I don't want to keep walking around like I'm okay with us just being business partners and friends, because I'm not." He doesn't react.

"So, what are you saying, Melody?" His words come out sternly. Still, I press on.

"I'm saying I want to be with you. I'm sure of it."

I reach for his hand, but he pulls back.

"Mel..." He stands. "I'm...I just don't know how to feel right now. What Natalie did fucked me up. This is all a lot, and I just need some time alone to process it."

He heads for the door. I follow, grabbing his hand before he reaches the handle.

"I know you're upset, but I need you to know that I'm sure about how I feel."

He turns, studying my face skeptically. "Are you?"

Before I can answer, he opens the door.

"I'll call you," he says, already stepping out.

The door shuts behind him.

And just like that, the tears come—hot and heavy—as the possibility settles in that I might just be too late.

My head is still pounding from the conversation I had with Mel last night. We didn't even get to talk about *us* because I was too consumed by what she told me about Natalie. Don't get me wrong—I understand Natalie being fed up with me, and I know I was 100% wrong in how I handled things with her. She was clear from the beginning about what she was looking for, and once I realized we weren't a good fit, I should've ended things. That part is on me.

But lying about being pregnant by me—then letting me carry the weight of that guilt—feels astronomically worse.

For a moment, I consider doing nothing at all. The easy thing would be to delete Natalie's number and pretend none of this ever happened. Act like she never existed. But that's not who I am. I've always dealt with shit head-on, even when it's uncomfortable. Especially then.

Before I can overthink it, Natalie's number is ringing on the other end of my phone. She picks up almost immediately.

"Tyrell. Hey. Listen, I—"

"Before you say anything, Natalie," I cut in, my frustration spilling over, "I need you to understand that what you did was incredibly fucked up! You lied about being pregnant with my child. You had me grieving a baby that was never even mine. You can say it was 'revenge' or whatever helps you sleep at night, but let me remind you that we were not in a committed relationship. We weren't even exclusive! And you know that—because you got knocked up by another nigga and tried to hold me responsible for it so I'd feel bad. That shit was uncalled for."

There's silence on the other end. When she finally speaks, her voice is so low that I can barely hear her.

"I know it was messed up, Ty, and I really am sorry. I never should've taken things this far. I was just...in my feelings. Seeing you talk about Melody, then hearing about you being out with her—it hurt."

I take a deep breath, forcing myself to calm down...The reality is, what's done is done. Dragging this out won't change anything.

"I get that you were frustrated," I say, my tone steadier now. "And you had every right to be upset with me. I handled things wrong. If I could go back and change how I moved, I would."

"I appreciate you saying that," she says softly. "I honestly don't know what else to say, except I'm sorry. I really hope you can forgive me."

"I have no choice but to forgive you, Nat," I admit. "I can't walk around carrying this level of anger and frustration. It's not good for me. Mentally, emotionally—it's not worth it."

I pause, taking another deep breath, grounding myself the way my therapist taught me years ago. At first, I thought the breathing exercises were bullshit. Turns out, they're the only reason I'm not losing my shit right now...

"I appreciate that," she says in a soft voice. "I really cared about you, Ty. I still do."

I bite back the urge to respond with something sharp. It wouldn't serve either of us.

"I know you did," I say instead. "Good luck with everything, Natalie. I wish you well."

I don't wait for her to respond before I hang up the phone.

I sink into the couch, waiting for the Tylenol I just downed to kick in. That was one of two phone calls I needed to make this morning.

The next is to Mel.

She's probably furious with me—and honestly, she has every right to be. I let my anger toward Natalie consume all my energy, leaving me with nothing left to deal with *us*. But avoiding Mel isn't an option. She's the woman I love, and fixing things between us matters more than anything else right now.

Calling her isn't enough.

I need to see her.

I head straight to the shower, throw on a hoodie and sweatpants, and grab my keys. This conversation can't wait any longer. I'm not giving myself time to second-guess it.

I'm going to her place.

Within the next thirty minutes, I'm standing in the lobby of Melody's apartment building, requesting to be let in. My heart is beating faster than it should be, palms slightly damp—something I don't usually feel. By the time the elevator doors open on her floor, I already know this conversation will change everything, one way or another.

I knock using the rhythm she's teased me about for years—*my* knock. The door opens, and there she is.

Melody stands in front of me, wearing a fluffy white robe, a towel wrapped around her head, brows furrowed as she takes me in. The look on her face tells me everything: she's surprised, confused, and definitely not expecting me at her door at 9:19 a.m. on a Thursday.

"Hey," I say gently. "Sorry to bother you. I know you're probably busy, but...Can I talk to you for a minute?"

"You must've forgotten how to use your phone," she says, already turning away. "You could've called."

She pads toward the bathroom, slippers flapping against the floor.

"Give me a minute. I'm in the middle of wash day."

I groan inwardly. I remember Melody's wash days from college—those weren't quick. And I don't have the luxury of waiting. Not today.

"I really need to talk to you, Mel," I say, following her into the en-suite. "This can't wait."

I sit on the closed toilet lid while she unwraps the towel and works product into her curls, rolling her eyes before a small smile creeps in.

"I see that," she says. "What's going on? You okay?"

"First, I want to apologize for how I left the other night," I say, cutting straight to it. "I was upset, and I didn't want to take that out on you. I needed to calm down before I said something I couldn't take back."

She turns to face me, curls framing her face.

"I understood why you were upset and needed some time. I'm not mad at that," she says quietly. "What I didn't under-stand was…When I finally told you I wanted to be with you, you asked me if I was sure."

She exhales, fingers fidgeting.

"I thought maybe you were tired of my back and forth. Maybe you were *done*."

"I *am* tired of the back and forth," I admit. "But that doesn't mean I want to give up. I came here because I want to figure out how we move forward—*together*."

Her shoulders slump just a little.

"I just…it's just been really hard for me to be in a space where I'm taking risks with someone I care so deeply about. The shit I went through with my mom last year damn near traumatized me, I think." She gives a small smile, like she's trying to convince herself she's okay, even as her eyes threaten to spill over.

Since I've known Melody, her relationship with her mother

has always been complicated. After her father passed away in that fatal car accident, her mom was left with survivor's guilt that never loosened its grip. She walked away from the crash with barely a scratch, while Keon—Mel's dad—died almost instantly.

After that, her mother turned to alcohol to cope with the grief and the guilt, and Melody was eventually raised by her uncle and grandmother. Over the years, Mel tried everything she could to help her mom—rehab, ultimatums, patience. At one point, her mom stayed sober for about three months. Then she relapsed, and the cycle started all over again.

Last year, I helped Melody look for her mom one afternoon. We found her drunk out of her mind, unsteady on her feet, anger and bitterness spilling out just as freely as the alcohol. She blamed Melody for her father's death. Blamed her for her own drinking. For everything.

I remember parts of that conversation like it just happened.

"Mom, please. Please let me get you some help. You don't have to live like this. I need you."
"It's your fault I'm like this in the first place! If you weren't crying for more snacks and shit, your daddy and I would've never gotten in that car. You did this to us! You did this to me!"
"I was just a kid, Mom! It wasn't my fault! Please just let me help you."
"I don't need your fucking help. Leave me the fuck alone!"
Through sobs, I watched Melody step toward her, trying to wrap her arms around her, trying to anchor her long enough to get her into the car. For a brief moment, her mom's eyes softened—just enough to give Melody hope. Then, she took another swig from the bottle and shook Mel off.
"Leave me the fuck alone. I'll get sober...when I'm ready."
"I love you, Mom. I need you."

*"Leave me alone, Melody. Don't come back out here lookin' for
me no more. It's not safe for you to be out here."*

Her mom turned and walked away.

*Melody didn't chase her. Didn't call after her. She just stood
there for a second, silent, before turning toward me. Her eyes were
red, her body shaking as she finally broke down. I pulled her into
my arms while she cried, holding her as tightly as I could. It took
a long time before she could even breathe normally again, let
alone get back into the car.*

*A tear slipped down my own face. I'd lost my mother too—under
completely different circumstances—but grief is grief. And I
understood, in that moment, that there were no words that could
fix what she was feeling. I promised myself then that whenever
she was ready to talk, whenever she needed someone, I would be
there. However she needed me to be.*

*We drove back to her apartment in silence, her face turned
toward the window the entire way. When we arrived, I walked
her upstairs, even though she insisted she was fine. I waited while
she showered, changed into her softest pajamas, and crawled
straight into bed.*

I thought she might wake up and want to talk.

She didn't.

And until now, she's never mentioned her mother again.

"Mel, you need to talk to someone about your mom and
how you're feeling. It doesn't have to be me, or Tisha, or your
uncle. You carry so much inside, and you don't have to do that
alone."

"I know," she says, releasing one of my hands to grab a
tissue. "I actually made an appointment to talk to a therapist. I
feel so many things all the time, and music and the gym are
really my only outlets. I didn't want to put my shit on my
friends or my family. I figured I could just...handle it alone."

"You shouldn't have to," I say gently. "Even with our privilege and our celebrity, we're still human. We still get hurt. You don't need to shoulder everything by yourself. Talking to someone will help you make sense of what you're feeling, instead of just surviving it."

She tilts her head, a playful smile tugging at her lips. "You sure you even want to be with me? I might be a little fucked up."

I don't smile back—not because I don't find her cute, but because I need her to hear me.

"I asked if you were sure out of anger, Melody. I didn't mean that shit. Not even a little. How I feel about you hasn't changed. I still want you. Very much."

Her expression softens, and she reaches up, her fingers brushing the side of my face.

"I'm really happy to hear that."

"So...are you done making me chase you?" I ask, half joking, half exhausted. "You're stressing me the fuck out."

Her smile fades, replaced with something quieter. More honest.

"To be real with you, Ty, I've been scared to lose you. Outside of my immediate family, you're the closest person to me. I'm not in the headspace to lose another person I love. That's why I've been pushing you away. I don't think I could handle us falling apart."

"Then we don't have to fall apart," I say, simply. "We can be together for as long as we choose to be. However long that is —that's our decision."

I pull her into my arms and kiss her forehead. Her eyes close, and I know she's sitting with everything—our history, the years we spent circling each other, and the reality of finally being here.

She looks up at me. "I'm ready to really do this, Ty. I just need you to be patient with me. If I shut down sometimes, it's not personal. I'll communicate as best as I can. But there are moments when I need space to sit with my feelings and process them."

"I know," I say softly. "We both got our shit. Be patient with me, and I'll be patient with you. And let's be honest—your mean ass wasn't gonna change overnight anyway."

I grin, fluffing at her curls.

"You really think I'm mean?"

"Only when you want to be," I say. "Most of the time, you're one of the sweetest people I know."

She leans in and presses a soft kiss to my lips.

"I think you're just trying to butter me up," she says, smiling wider than she probably has in days.

"Absolutely," I reply. "I'm ready to see what's under this robe."

She laughs and swats at me before turning back to her hair. Apparently, I'm not allowed to interfere with wash day—or risk "messing up the routine." I settle back onto the closed toilet lid, watching my now-girlfriend move around the bathroom, chatting about products and plans like the world hasn't just shifted.

I don't complain. Instead, I opt for watching her in admiration.

I've waited fifteen years for this moment.

I wake up Friday morning to the sound of a delivery alert on my phone. After yesterday's emotionally charged conversation with Ty—followed by spending the entire day together and hours of lovemaking—I am completely drained. I kicked him out last night so I'd have enough energy to make it to the gym this morning. He put up a little fight about leaving, until I reminded him that neither one of us would get any real rest if he stayed a minute longer.

I throw on my robe and slippers and make my way to the front door.

"Just a minute!" I call out. "Who's there?"

"Delivery for Ms. Ford," a chipper male voice responds from the other side.

I open the door to see a floral arrangement so massive, the delivery man has to peek around it just to show me his face.

"Oh, my goodness! Thank you!"

"You're welcome, ma'am. If you could just sign here."

I scribble my signature on the receipt and carefully lift the heavy bouquet from his arms.

"You must be very special to someone," he says with a smile.

I thank him again and close the door with my foot, needing both hands to keep from dropping the arrangement. I already know who it's from. The thought alone makes me blush as I search for the card tucked between the flowers.

Melody,

Thank you for agreeing to trust me with your heart. I promise to take care of it the best way that I can.

I loved you then.

I love you now.

I'll love you forever.

With adoration,

Tyrell

A Song for You: Frankie Beverly & Maze- "Can't Get Over You"

P.S. Thanks for the lesson on patience. 15 years was a stretch tho. :)

I shake my head, smiling to myself. I can't believe this is really happening. All the *what ifs* I buried over the years—the quiet hope that Tyrell and I might one day find our way here—finally have room to exist.

He's allowing them to grow.

And maybe for the first time, I am too.

I know navigating this new space won't always be easy, especially as we continue chasing our careers and our individual dreams. But, I'm done obsessing over what could go wrong. I refuse to live like that anymore.

Instead, I pick up my phone.

> Morning, Sweetie. Thank you for the flowers. I love them!

TY

You're welcome, babe. I wanted them to reach you before you left for the gym.

> I'm on a high now. I don't think I need the gym anymore lol.

TY

You rode dick for 10 minutes last night, and now you're ready to quit working out? Ain't that some shit! 😅

> 😅😅😅 Fuck you.

TY

Love you too.

> Call you when I'm done. I wrote a couple of songs that I want us to work on later.

TY

You wrote songs about me already? You really do love me.

> All my songs have been about you, Ty.

TY

You're making me blush.

> Whatever! We'll talk later. I love you.

TY

I love you more.

CHAPTER 55

Tyrell

I am signaled to begin reading the teleprompter in three... two...one.

"Welcome to *Notes of Passion*, a card game designed to spark intimate conversations between couples. My name is Tyrell, and some of you might know me from the R&B group, *Mel & Ty*. Now, I know you're probably wondering what I'm doing here, considering I've never publicly spoken about being in a relationship. Well..." I pause briefly, smiling. "My dating life recently got an upgrade. I figured I'd come on here and show y'all how to play this game with someone very special to me."

The camera pans to Melody, seated across from me, smiling and waving.

"Hey y'all. I know what some of you are thinking—and trust me, it's a long story."

"A fifteen-year-long story," I interject, earning a laugh from her. I gesture to the deck of *Notes of Passion* cards and pull the first one. "You ready for this, Mel?"

She takes a breath. "I think so. I'm a little scared, honestly. I don't know what kind of questions are on these cards, and my grandmother might be watching."

We both laugh as I read the first question aloud.

"Alright. First question. Ooh—this is a good one. *What is a non-sexual thing about me that turns you on?*"

Melody tilts her head, thinking.

"Your passion for your craft," she says, finally. "The way you'll sit at your piano for hours, working through whatever melodies are in your head. I love watching you create." She pauses, then laughs softly. "It's honestly the only time you're ever serious."

I grin at her. "So basically, I've been sitting at my piano turning you on since we were nineteen."

"That's what you took from that?" She shakes her head, laughing, then pulls her own card. Her eyes widen as she reads it before she throws her head back, laughing again. "This one is...very personal, babe."

"Go for it."

"Okay. You asked for it." She reads aloud. "*Rate our sex life on a scale from one to ten, with ten being the highest. What, if anything, can I improve on?*"

"Ten out of ten," I answer immediately. "No notes."

"No notes?" she presses. "There has to be *something*. Or are you just extremely satisfied?"

"More than satisfied, baby." I wink, and she leans forward to slap my leg.

"This is so embarrassing!" she laughs.

"Don't be embarrassed. You should be proud of your skills."

"Tyrell, please. Let's move on."

The entire production team laughs along with us. I take the hint and pull another card.

"Okay, Mel. This one says: *What is a secret you think I'm keeping from you?*"

Her posture straightens. "I'm glad you asked." She smiles, knowingly. "A while ago, you went to my uncle's house and had a conversation with him that he still refuses to tell me about. I wanna know what that was about."

"Are you serious?" I laugh. "I really just went to him for advice and to talk about a few things."

"About...?" She arches a brow.

"About your stubborn ass," I say, turning toward the camera. "This was back when Melody was paying me dust, y'all. I was trying, and she was shutting me down every chance she got. I needed guidance."

"And the *few* things?" she presses.

"You really want to know?" I meet her eyes, my tone shifting.

"I do," she says, just as serious.

"I went to your uncle to tell him my intentions with you," I say. "I wanted him to know that I was serious—that when, not if, we finally got it together, I would do right by you."

"And...?" she whispers.

I smile. "And I asked for his blessing, because I fully intend to make you my wife someday."

Her eyes glisten immediately. I reach across the space between us, take her hand, and press a kiss to it before resting it back in her lap.

She looks at me with a softness I've waited years to see.

"I love you," she says quietly.

"I love you more."

For a moment, we just sit there, locked in each other's gaze, forgetting entirely where we are. It isn't until someone from production waves a cue card at me that I realize our silence has gone on a little too long.

I clear my throat, reaching for another card with a grin. "Alright. Enough of the sentimental, lovey-dovey stuff. Let's get back to the freaky shit."

Melody laughs, shaking her head as we continue the game—no longer hiding, no longer denying, no longer afraid to admit our love for one another to ourselves, and to the world.

1 Year Later

It's a warm Friday night in July, and Tyrell and I are celebrating our first anniversary.

He reserved a table at a new rooftop restaurant in downtown LA, with an indoor dining area below. Tyrell looks dangerously handsome in a tailored plum-colored suit, a crisp white button-down, black loafers, and a black handkerchief embroidered with subtle plum, red, and white details. I hadn't planned to dress up this much—but when he showed up at my door earlier, locs cascading down his back, hairline and beard freshly groomed, looking like *that*, I changed my mind immediately.

I swap my casual summer dress for a black sleeveless number with ruffles and an asymmetrical slit. The neckline dips just enough to show the outline of my breasts—something Tyrell has never once complained about. I finish the look with gold and diamond jewelry and a pair of gold René Caovilla wraparound sandals that Ty bought me last year. My hair is swept into a Beyoncé *B'Day*-inspired updo, curls framing my face.

As I apply the final swipe of lip gloss, I hear him call out,

"Mel, are you almost ready? We're gonna be late."

Tyrell may be unserious about many things, but punctuality is not one of them. I've learned that over the last year—ten minutes late might as well be an hour in his mind.

"I'm coming!" I rush out of the closet to find him pacing near the kitchen. The tension in his face melts the second he sees me.

"You look beautiful, babe."

His compliments still make me blush. "Thank you, sweetie. Let's go before you have a medical emergency over us being late." I pause. "Oh—wait. I got you a gift. I want you to see it now."

"Leave it here," he says. "We'll exchange gifts later."

"You sure?"

"Yes, Mel." His tone is already shifting back to urgency. "I've got something for you, too. Now let's go."

I laugh. "Okay, okay. I'm coming."

At the restaurant, I immediately notice the sign at the front desk: **Rooftop Closed for Private Event**.

"Oh," I say, disappointment slipping out before I can stop it. "The rooftop's closed tonight." Ty sold me on the rooftop and how nice it was, even making me promise I wouldn't look it up, so I could be surprised.

Tyrell frowns. "Damn. I didn't know that." He scans the room. "Let me talk to someone—see if we can at least go up there for a minute."

"It's fine," I say quickly, squeezing his hand. "We'll do another rooftop another time."

He's already half-distracted, taking in the space.

"This place is beautiful," I say, marveling at the décor myself.

"Yeah, it's really nice. I just hope the food is good. I'm so hungry, I could eat anything right about now."

I raise an eyebrow, a devious smirk on display.

"Later." We both laugh at the unspoken innuendo between us, and Tyrell squeezes my hand as we are led by a hostess to our table.

We are seated at our table, sifting through our menus when the waiter brings us the bottle of wine Tyrell ordered. He raises his glass up to clink with mine in a toast, eyes filled with the sincerity and passion I've grown so used to seeing from him. My eyes meet his, and I hope they convey the same passion.

"Cheers to us, Mel. We've come a long way." He pauses, then adds with a grin, "I'm glad you finally let me hit it."

I laugh. "Wow. I see you decided to lay the romance on thick tonight."

He takes my hand. "You know I love you more than anything and anyone in the world. I'm so glad we took a chance on us. Best decision I ever made."

His words make me blush, and I can't downplay the effect he has on me.

"I'm so glad I got my shit together," I admit. "I dodged you for a long time—but we both knew I wouldn't last."

"I love you," he says softly.

"I love you more."

He keeps staring at me, intensity flickering behind his eyes.

"What?" I ask. "Why are you looking at me like that?"

"Just admiring you," he says. "You somehow get more beautiful every day. It's stressful."

Jokingly, he takes his table napkin and pretends to frantically pat his face dry.

"You are so silly. But I don't know about that. I was pretty hot in college."

"Yeah," he says. "But you didn't have all that ass back then."

I hit him with my own napkin, and we both erupt in laughter, only to be interrupted by our waiter.

"Good news," the waiter says. "My manager has just let me know that we are inviting special guests up to the rooftop before the private event starts. If you'd still like to see it, the host can show you up. We have a full bar as well. Please have a drink on me to celebrate your anniversary."

"Oh my God, thank you so much!" I beam. "We appreciate that. I was really upset that I wouldn't get to see it. I've heard so many good things about it."

"Yeah, it's really nice," he says. "You get a view of most of downtown LA. Glad I could help you all with this."

Tyrell stands, shaking our waiter's hand.

"Thanks, man. We really appreciate it. We'll definitely be back here."

A host leads us up to the roof and suggests I check out the ladies' room, which she shares has a great mirror for selfies. I excuse myself to the bathroom.

"I'll wait for you by the bar," Tyrell lets me know.

The rooftop is expansive, decorated with beautiful floral arrangements. The sounds of a band playing soft R&B music fills my ears, and I hum along to their rendition of Tony! Toni! Tone!'s "Anniversary" as I fix my hair in the bathroom mirror and reapply my lip combo.

Satisfied with how I look, I head out of the bathroom area. I hear a voice that sounds oddly familiar singing Stevie Wonder's *Ribbon In The Sky.* "That guy sounds exactly like Uncle Keith," I say to myself, eager to get to where the band is so I can record a video to send my uncle.

I walk to where I hear the music, immediately taking in the decor around me. There are adornments of red roses lined throughout the rooftop, with what seems like hundreds of candles neatly scattered around. Paired with the evening sky highlighting all of the beauty of downtown LA, the scenery feels ethereal.

As beautiful as the rooftop is decorated, however, my attention is on the man in the plum colored suit with the locs hanging down in his face, eyes focused on me, down on one knee, a small black box in his hand.

Tears immediately fill my eyes, and I walk towards Tyrell, guided by our same waiter from earlier.

"Melody," he says, voice steady. "I've been in love with you since I was nineteen. I've loved every part of our journey—but I don't want it to continue without you as my wife." He swallows. "I love you more than you could ever imagine. Will you marry me?"

I nod before I can even speak.

"Yes!"

I manage to get the word out through my tears. He slips the ring onto my finger and stands, pulling me into his arms. His kiss steals the breath from my lungs.

"I love you," I whisper.

"I love you more."

We stare at each other for a few seconds before he grins.

"Now come see this overpriced band that your uncle put together. He didn't even give me the family discount."

"You're so stupid!" I laugh, gripping his hand while we

walk to greet our friends and family. Before we make it over to where the band is, Tyrell stops me.

"I would've waited fifteen more years for you, you know that?"

I smile, heart full. "I would've waited forever."

Acknowledgments

This story started as just a few scenes that I wrote down in my Notes app a year ago, unsure of what I could even do with them. I'd write, feel good about it, then let fear, uncertainty (and a hint of imposter syndrome) make me feel like I had no business trying to write anything at all. '*This Song Is For You*' was truly a labor of love, and I have to say—I'm so glad I didn't give up on it.

There are so many people who aided in this process and helped me take my ideas from iPhone to print.

To my editor (and Twin), Ena Coleman: I can't thank you enough for your guidance, wisdom, and support during this process. You went above and beyond for me, and it doesn't go unnoticed. We're locked in forever!

To 'The Writer's Room': Carolyn, Janeé, and Jasmine, Thank you for responding in the group chat every time, for taking the time out to read whatever I emailed you at whatever time I emailed it, giving me feedback, and for making me feel like I could really do this. I love y'all!

To Johnathan Lawrence and Natasha Small-Isaac: Thank you both so much for your tech support and all of your help during this process. I'd still be trying to use the free version of LemonSqueezy without you two, lol.

To Mae Rose: Thank you for making me such a beautiful cover in what feels like record timing. You really brought my vision to life.

To all my friends and family: Thank you for the encouragement and for your constant cheers along the way. It is from watching you all confidently live and flourish in your journeys that I've been able to walk in mine.

To the readers: I am deeply appreciative of all of the support from each and every one of you. Thank you for affirming that I belong in this space, for pouring into me, and for the genuine kindness you've shown. I hope this is just the beginning of our relationship.

And finally,

To my Sweeties, Aiden and Olivia: Neither one of you is allowed to read this until you're at least 40, but I hope seeing your mom pursue her passion inspires you to do the same. Even if you're scared, listen to that voice inside of you telling you to use your gifts. And when you use them, do so to the best of your ability. I love you.

A lover of all things romance with a commitment to celebrating Black stories, D. Michelle is a proud native New Yorker that loves, love. She's a mom constantly balancing career, her love of reading and music, and all her many interests. Living in Brooklyn, NY, she can often be found having "something sweet" after a good meal and curling up with a good book—or staying up to write her next one.

Connect with D. Michelle!

Website: dmichellewrites.com

TikTok: tiktok.com/dmichellewrites

Instagram: instagram.com/dmichellewrites

www.ingramcontent.com/pod-product-compliance
Lightning Source LLC
Chambersburg PA
CBHW030428160726
47991CB00005B/1642